Marjorie's Maytime

Carolyn Wells

TABLE OF CONTENTS

CHAPTER I
A MAY PARTY

"Marjorie Maynard's May
Came on a beautiful day;
  And Marjorie's Maytime
  Is Marjorie's playtime;
And that's what I sing and I say!
    Hooray!
Yes, that's what I sing and I say!"

Marjorie was coming downstairs in her own sweet way, which was accomplished by putting her two feet close together, and jumping two steps at a time. It didn't expedite her descent at all, but it was delightfully noisy, and therefore agreeable from Marjorie's point of view.

The May-day was undeniably beautiful. It was warm enough to have doors and windows flung open, and the whole house was full of May that had swarmed in from out of doors.

The air was soft and fragrant, the leaves were leaving out, the buds were budding, and the spring was springing everywhere.

The big gold bushes of the Forsythia were masses of yellow bloom; crocuses popped up through the grass; a few birds had begun to sing, and the sun shone as if with a settled determination to push the spring ahead as fast as he could.

Moreover it was Saturday, which was the best proof of all, of an intelligent and well-behaved Spring. For a May-day which knew enough to fall on a Saturday was a satisfactory May-day, indeed!

Of course there was to be a May party, and of course it was to be at the Maynards', because Marjorie always claimed that the whole month of May belonged to their family, and she improved every shining hour of the Maytime.

The May party was really under the auspices of the Jinks Club. But as the club was largely composed of Maynards, it was practically a Maynard May party.

The bowers for the May Queens had been built out on the lawn, and though a little wabbly as to architecture, they were beautiful of decoration, and highly satisfactory to the Royalty most interested.

There were two May Queens, because Marjorie and Delight both wanted the position; and though both were willing to resign in favor of the other it was a much pleasanter arrangement to have two Queens. So there were two bowers, and Marjorie was to be the Red Queen and Delight the White Queen.

Of course Kingdon was the May King. No one had ever heard of a May King before, but that didn't bother the Jinks Club any, for they were a law unto themselves.

Kitty and Dorothy Adams were Princesses of May, and Flip Henderson was a Prince of May. Rosy Posy was a May Maid of Honor, and Mrs. Maynard was persuaded to accept the role of Queen Dowager of May.

Miss Hart was of the party, and the title of Duchess of May seemed to fit her exactly.

And now the time had come, and Marjorie was jumping downstairs on her way to her own coronation. She wore a red dress, very much trimmed with flowers made of red tissue paper. The name of the flower doesn't matter, for they were not exact copies of nature, but they were very pretty and effective, and red silk stockings and slippers finished off the brilliant costume that was very becoming to Marjorie's rosy face, with its dark eyes and dark curly hair.

As she reached the lower hall she saw Delight coming across the street, arrayed as the White Queen. Really she looked more like a fairy, with her frilly white frock and her golden hair and blue eyes.

"Hello, Flossy Flouncy!" called out King, using his pet name for Delight; "you're a daisy May Queen! I offer you my humble homage!"

A daisy May Queen was an appropriate term, for Delight's white frock was trimmed and wreathed with garlands of daisies. Not real ones, for they were not yet in bloom, except in green-houses; and so artificial ones had been sewn on her frock with pretty effect.

King's own attempt at a regal costume had resulted gorgeously, for with his mother's help, he had contrived a robe of state, which looked like purple velvet and ermine, though it was really canton flannel. But it had a grand and noble air, and King wore it with a majestic strut that would have done credit to any coronation.

Kitty and Dorothy wore light green dresses trimmed with pink paper roses, and were very pretty little princesses; while Rosy Posy as Maid of Honor wore one of her own little white frocks, tied up lavishly with blue ribbons.

Flip Henderson's costume was a good deal like King's, as he had purposely copied it, not having any other design to work from.

Mrs. Maynard and Miss Hart were not so fancifully attired as the younger members of the party, but they wore pretty light gowns with more or less floral decoration.

The whole affair was impromptu; the children had spent the morning getting it up, and now were going to devote the afternoon to the party itself.

"We must make a procession," began Marjorie, who was mistress of ceremonies; "you must go first, Mother, because the May Queen Dowager is the most honorable one."

"Me go first, too," announced Rosy Posy, taking her mother's hand.

"Yes, you may," said Marjorie. "In fact, Baby, you'd better go first of all, because you're Maid of Honor; and so you walk in front of the Queen Dowager."

So Rosy Posy toddled ahead, followed by Mrs. Maynard, who carried a wand of flowers with gracious effect.

"The Queens ought to come next," said King, but Marjorie's sense of politeness interfered with this plan.

"No, the Duchess must come next," she said; "I don't care whether it's right or not as a procession, but I think Miss Hart ought to go before us children."

So the Duchess of May took her place next in line, and then the two Queens side by side followed.
Then came the two Princesses, and behind them, the King of May and the Prince, walking together in affable companionship. It was an imposing sight, and the paraders were so pleased with themselves that they marched round the lawn several times before going to the scene of the festivity.

But at last they went to the Coronation Bowers, and decided it was time for the ceremonies to begin.

The two crowns were in readiness for the two Queens. They were exactly alike, and were made of pasteboard covered with gilt paper. Miss Hart had helped with these, and they were really triumphs of gorgeous beauty. Each lay on a lace-trimmed cushion, and with them were long golden sceptres with gilt balls on top.

"Who's to do to the crowning?" asked King.

"Why, I supposed you had those details all settled in advance," said Miss Hart, laughing.
"No," returned King, "we didn't fix things up ahead much, we thought we'd just make up as we went along. I'll crown Flossy Flouncy, and Flip, you crown Marjorie,—that'll be all right."

The other members of the Royal Family took seats on rustic benches, and the two Queens mounted their thrones. The bowers were pretty, and as they stood side by side, framing the smiling Queens, it was a pretty picture.

"I hate to stop the proceedings," said Miss Hart, "but I think I must run over and get my camera, and take a snap-shot of this Coronation."

"All right," said King, agreeably, "we'll wait. We'll sing a song while you're gone, and you can skip over and back in no time."

So while the children sang the "Star Spangled Banner," Miss Hart ran across the street, and came back with her camera.

"Better wait until they get their crowns on," suggested Kitty, "they'll look a heap queenlier then."

3

So the coronation ceremony proceeded. The King and the Prince advanced majestically to the thrones, bearing the crowns on their cushions.

"Who'll make the speech?" asked the King.

"You may," said Flip, politely.

"No, you're better at it than I am. Well, we'll each make one. You can begin."

So Flip advanced, and holding his burden high at arms' length he dropped on one knee before Marjorie, and began to declaim in oratorical tones:

"Fair Maiden, Queen of May, I salute thee! I salute all the rest of you too, but mostly the Queen, because she is the principal pebble on the beach. Queens always are. And so, Fair Maiden, Fair Maynard Maiden, I salute thee."

"That's enough saluting," put in King; "go on with your crowning."

"And so, fair Queen of May, I crown thee, our Queen and our Sovereign! May your shadow never grow less, and may you have many happy returns of the day! And with kind regards to all, I'm your humble servant."

Having set the crown squarely on Marjorie's head, Flip bowed low in humble salutation, and then resumed an upright position, rather pleased with his own speech.

"I accept thy homage, O Prince," said Marjorie, as she bowed and smiled with queenly grace; "and I shall endeavor to be the best Queen in all the world, except Delight, who will probably be better."

With this graceful tribute to her companion queen, Marjorie sat down, holding her head very straight lest her crown should tumble off.

Then King advanced to Delight, and holding up the other crown, began his declamatory effort.

"Oh, Queen! Oh, White Queen! Oh, our beautiful sovereign! I bring to thee a crown,—a crown to crown you with, to show to all that you are our beloved and beloving Queen of May. Accept, oh, Queen, this crown and sceptre, and with them the assurance of our alleged loyalty, our humble submission, and our majestic royalty! I am a little at a loss for any thing further to say, as I can't think of any more highfalutin words, so you may as well put on your crown, and let's have some fun."

But though King's high-flown language failed him, it was with a very magnificent manner that he crowned his Queen and gave her the flower-trimmed sceptre.

Then Delight, looking lovelier than ever in her added regalia, made her own little speech.

"I thank you, my people, for your tokens of love and loyalty. I thank you for choosing me to be your queen, and my rule shall be a happy one. My only law is, for everybody to do just what they want to, and so I pronounce the Coronation Ceremonies over."

Delight bowed, and sat down on her throne, while the audience applauded heartily.

Then the two Queens came down from their bowers, and Royalty gave way to the members of the Jinks Club.

"Now, let's cut up jinks!" cried King, capering about in his long Court robes, and looking like a very merry Monarch, indeed. "First the May-pole dance, that'll limber us up some."

A May-pole had been erected near by, and from its top depended long ribbons of various colors. Each of the party took one of these ribbons, and under the direction of Miss Hart, they danced round the May-pole, weaving the ribbons in and out. It was a complicated matter at first, but they soon learned how, and wove and unwove the ribbons many times without getting tangled once. As they danced, they sang a little May song that Miss Hart had taught them, and as they danced faster and faster it became a frolic rather than a dignified rite.

At last, all out of breath they dropped on the grass, and begged Miss Hart to tell them a story.

"I'll tell you of the origin of the May-day celebrations," she said. "May-day has been a festival since very ancient times. Its reason for being is the natural feeling that comes to every one at the glad spring time. When Nature breaks out into new life and beauty, our hearts feel a sympathetic gladness, and a celebration of the spring is the natural outcome. The most primitive people felt this inclination, and they used to gather the flowers that bloomed in profusion about them, set them up, and to pay them a sort of homage, expressed in dance and song. The old Romans had what they called Floralia, or Floral Games, which began on the twenty-eighth of April, and lasted several days. Later in England, and especially in the Middle Ages, it was the custom for people of all ranks, even the Court itself, to go out early in the morning on the first of May and gather flowers. Especially did they gather hawthorn, and huge branches of this flower were brought home about sunrise, with accompaniments of pipe and tabor, and much joy and merriment. Then the people decorated their houses with the flowers they had brought. And because of this, they called this ceremony bringing Home the May, or going A-Maying, and so the hawthorn bloom itself acquired the name of May, and is often spoken of by that name. In those early days, the fairest maid of the village was crowned with flowers, and called the Queen of May; she sat in state in a little bower or arbor while her youthful courtiers danced and sang around her. But the custom of having a May Queen really dates back to the old Roman celebration when they especially worshipped the goddess Flora. Another feature of May-day was the May-pole, which was erected in all English towns and villages, and round which the people danced all day long. But these merry customs were stopped when the Puritans put an end to all such jollifications. They were revived somewhat after the restoration, but they are rarely seen nowadays except among children. But they are all pretty customs, and the whole subject will well repay reading and study. I won't continue this lecture now, but before the month of May is over, we will study in school hours some of its characteristics, and we will read the poem of the May Queen, by Lord Tennyson."

"I wish you had boys in your school, Miss Hart," said Flip Henderson; "you do teach the nicest way I ever heard of."

"Indeed she does," agreed Marjorie; "going to school to Miss Hart is like going to a party every day."

And then came the crowning glory of the May party. This was the feast, which was served out of doors on a table prettily decorated with vines and flowers. Dainty sandwiches were tied up with pink ribbons, and little glass cups held delicious pink lemonade. The cakes were iced with pink, the ice cream was pink, and there were pink bon-bons of various sorts. At each plate was a little pink box of candies to take home; and a souvenir for each guest in the shape of a pink fan for the girls, and pink balloons for the boys. The big balloons made much fun as they bobbed about in the air, and when the feast was over, the guests went away declaring that the Jinks Club had never had a prettier party.

CHAPTER II
A NEW PET

When Mr. Maynard came home that night he was treated to an account of the whole affair, but as two or three of the little Maynards often talked at once, the effect was sometimes unintelligible.

"It was the loveliest party, Father," said Marjorie, as she hung over one arm of his chair, and arranged a somewhat large bunch of blossoms in his buttonhole.

"Yes, it was," agreed Kitty, who hung on the other arm of the chair, and investigated his coat pockets in the hope of finding a box of candy or other interesting booty.

"It sure was!" declared King, who was sitting on a footstool near, and hugging one knee with apparently intense affection.

"And what made it so especially delightful?" asked Mr. Maynard, as he balanced Rosy Posy on his knee; "you tell me, Baby."

"It was a bootiful party," said Rosy Posy, with decision, "because we had pink ice cream."

"That was about the best part," said Kitty, reminiscently.

"Well, the pink ice cream part sounds delightful, I'm sure; but what was the rest of the party about?"

"Oh, it was a May party," exclaimed Marjorie, "and we had May Queens, and a May King, and May Princesses, and everything! I do love May, don't you, Father? Everything is so bright and bloomy and Maysy. I think it is the loveliest month in the year."

"Yes, it is a lovely month, Mopsy, and a good month to be out of doors.
Maytime is playtime."
"Yes, I know it; I made a song this morning about that. I'll sing it to you." And Marjorie sang for her father the little verse she had mad about Marjorie Maynard's May.

"Huh!" said King, "'tisn't your May, any more than anybody else's, Midget Maynard."

"No, I know it; but I like to think the May just belongs to us Maynards. Anyway we have it all. It is our May even if other people use it, too."

"I don't begrudge them the use of it," said Kitty; "of course, it's just as much theirs as ours."

"Yes, of course," assented Marjorie; "I'm only just sort of imagining, you know."

"Let me help you imagine, Midget," said her father. "How would you like to imagine a whole May time that was all playtime?"

"For all of us?" rejoined Marjorie, her eyes dancing. "Oh, that would be a lovely imagination! It would be like an Ourday all the time! And by the way, Father, you owe us an extra Ourday. You know we skipped one when you and Mother were down South, and it's time for another anyway. Shall we have two together?"

"Two together!" cried King; "what fun that would be! We could go off on a trip or something."

"Where could we stay all night?" asked Kitty, who was the practical one.

"Oh, trips always have places to stay all night," declared King; "let's do it, Father. What do you say?"

"I don't get a chance to say much of anything, among all you chatter-boxes. Rosy Posy, what do you say?"

But the littlest Maynard was so nearly asleep that she had no voice in the matter under consideration, and at her father's suggestion, Nurse Nannie came and took her away to bed.

"Now," said Mr. Maynard, "what's all this about Ourday? And two of them together! When do you think I'm going to get my business done?"

"Well, but, Father, you owe them to us," said Marjorie, patting his cheek in her wheedlesome way. "And you're not the kind of a business man who doesn't pay his debts, are you?"

"I hope not; that would be a terrible state of affairs! And so I owe you two Ourdays, do I?"

"Yes, one for April, and one for May."

It was the custom in the Maynard household to have an Ourday each month. On these occasions both Mr. and Mrs. Maynard devoted themselves all day long to the entertainment of the four children, and the four took turns in deciding what the nature of the entertainment should be. Much of the previous month their parents had been away, and the children looked forward to the celebration of the belated Ourday in connection with the one that belonged to the month of May.

"Before we discuss the question further," said Mr. Maynard, "I must tell you of something I did to-day. I adopted a new pet."

"Oh, Father, what is it—a dog?" cried Marjorie.

"No, it isn't a dog; guess again."

"A cat!" Kitty guessed, while King said, "A goat?"

"Wrong, all of you," said Mr. Maynard; "now see if you can't guess it by asking twenty questions."

"All right," said Marjorie, who was always ready for a game. "Is it animal, vegetable, or mineral?"

"All three; that is, it belongs to all three kingdoms."

"Is it a house?" asked Kitty.

"No, it is not as big as a house."

"Is it useful or ornamental?" asked King.

"Both; but its principal use is to give pleasure."

"How lovely!" cried Marjorie. "I guess it's a fountain! Oh, Father, where are you going to put it—on the side lawn? And will it have goldfish in it, and shiny stones, and green water plants growing in it?"

"Wait a minute, Mops; don't go so fast! You see, it isn't a fountain, and if you should put water and goldfish in it, you'd spoil it entirely."

"And any way, Father," said King, "you said it was a pet, didn't you?"

"Yes, my boy, a sort of pet."

"Can it talk?"

"No, it can't talk."

"Oh, I made sure it was a talking machine. What kind of a sound does it make?"

"Well, it purrs sometimes."

"Then it is a kitten after all," cried Kitty.

"No, it isn't a kitten. It's bigger than a kitten."

"An old cat!" said Marjorie, scornfully.

"Pooh," said King, "we'll never get at it this way. Of course it isn't a cat! Father wouldn't make so much fuss over just a cat."

"But I'm not making a fuss," protested Mr. Maynard; "I only told you I had adopted a new pet, and suggested you guess what it is. If you give up I'll tell you."

"I don't give up," cried Kitty; "what color is it?"

"Red," answered her father.

"Ho!" cried Kitty, with a sudden flash of inspiration, "it's an automobile!"

"Right you are, Kitsie," said her father, "though I don't know why you guessed it so quick."

"Well, nothing else is red and big. But why do you call it a pet? And how does it purr?"

"You're so practical, Kitty, it's difficult to make you understand; but I feel quite sure we'll all make a pet of it, and when you once hear it purr, you'll think it a prettier sound than any kitten ever made."

"Is it really an automobile, Father? And have you bought it? And shall we ride in it? Where is it? Where are you going to keep it? When will it come? How many will it hold? Where shall we ride first?"

These queries were flung at Mr. Maynard by the breathless children without waiting for answers, and as Mrs. Maynard came in just then, Mr. Maynard told the story of his new acquisition.

"I've been looking at them for some time, as you know, Helen," he said, looking at his wife, "and to-day I decided upon the purchase. It's a big touring car, and will comfortably accommodate the whole Maynard family and a chauffeur beside. It will arrive day after to-morrow, that's Monday, and after a few short spins around this neighborhood, I think by Thursday we may be able to start for an Ourday trip in it."

"A whole Ourday in an automobile!" cried Marjorie; "how gorgeous and grand! Oh, King, isn't it just splendiferous!"

Marjorie sprang to her feet, and grasped her brother round the neck, and they flew round the room in a sort of a wild Indian war-dance that went far to express their joy and delight at the prospect.

"Two Ourdays, you know, Father," said Kitty, nestling quietly to her father's side as her madcap brother and sister whirled round the room. But they brought up with a round turn, though a little dishevelled-looking, to hear Mr. Maynard's reply to Kitty's remark.

9

"Yes, two Ourdays at once!" Marjorie cried, affectionately pulling King's hair as she spoke. He returned the caress by pinching her ear, and said, "Will it be two Ourdays together, Father, or one at a time?"

"If you two young tornadoes will sit down quietly for a moment, you may hear of something to your advantage," said Mr. Maynard, smiling at his two eldest children who were rather red-faced and breathless from their recent exertions.

"Sure we will!" cried King, and drawing Marjorie down with him, they fell in a heap on the floor, and sat there awaiting further disclosures.

"You see," Mr. Maynard began, "as Marjorie says, Maytime is,—what?"

"Playtime," supplemented Marjorie, quickly.

"Well, then, if Maytime is playtime for the Maynards, why shouldn't we play all through the month of May?"

"Play every day,
All the month of May,
All the Maynards may
Play all day!
Hooray! Hooray! Hooray!"
sang Marjorie who often improvised her songs as she went along. This was not a difficult one to learn, and King and Kitty took up the refrain, and they sang it over and over with great gusto, until Mrs. Maynard begged for a respite.

"But of course you don't mean anything like that?" said Kitty, when the song had ceased.

"But that's just exactly what I do mean. What do you think of the plan of the Maynards going a-Maying in their own motor car, and taking the whole month of May for it?"

Marjorie's eyes opened wide. "I know what you mean!" she exclaimed; "you mean a tour—a tour through the country in an automobile! I've heard of such things!"

"Wise child!" said her father; "well, that's exactly what I do mean. A tour through the country in our own motor, and in our own Maytime. How does it strike you?"

"It strikes me all of a heap!" cried Marjorie, throwing herself into her father's arms; "tell me more, quick! Seems as if I can't believe it!"

"I can't believe it, either," said Kitty, slowly; "but I 'spect I can by the time we get ready to start. When are we going, Father?"

"On Thursday, if Mother can be ready."

"Oh, yes, I can be ready. I've only to get a few things for the children and myself to wear on the journey."

10

"Yes, we must all have up-to-date motor togs, I'm sure," and Mr. Maynard looked about as happy over the projected trip, as any of his children.

"But, Father," said Marjorie, "how can you take so much time away from your business? You said you couldn't take two Ourdays together because you were busy."

"I didn't say exactly that, dearie, and anyway I was only joking, because I knew I was going to spring this surprise on you in a few minutes. I have arranged, of course, to be away from my business for nearly a month, and have planned to spend the greater part of May taking this motor trip. We will go to Grandma Sherwood's first, and stay a few days,—"

"To Grandma Sherwood's? Oh, glorious!" And again Marjorie was seized with a paroxysm of joy, and this time she caught Kitty, and led her off for a mad dance round the room. "Just think of it, Kit," she cried, "we'll be at Grandma Sherwood's together, and you can see the lovely room she fixed up for me, and the house in the tree, and everything. Oh, Kitty!"

"But I'm going to be there all summer, anyway," said Kitty, as she finally induced Marjorie to tumble on the divan amid a heap of sofa pillows.

"Yes, I know; but that's different. But what fun for us all to be there together for a few days! Did you say a few days, Father?"

"Yes, I did; but if you're so turbulent, and excitable, and noisy I think a few hours'll be enough for Grandma and Uncle Steve."

"It may be enough for Grandma, but it won't for Uncle Steve," declared
Marjorie; "he loves rackety-packety children!"
"Well, he'll get his desires fulfilled when you get there," said Mrs. Maynard, smiling; "but perhaps the trip there will calm you down a little bit."

"No, it won't! It just makes me more and more crazy all the time I think of it! Oh, Father, won't we have a lot of our Ourdays all at once!"

"Indeed we will, enough to last for several years ahead. For if you debit me with last month's deficiency, of course you must credit me in the future."

"Oh, no, this rule doesn't work both ways! We'll just take all the Ourdays that we can get whenever we can get them. But what are we going to do after we leave Grandma's?"

"Well, if you all agree, I thought we might go over to New York and see your other grandma."

"Go to Grandma Maynard's, too! Oh, what fun we will have!" and Marjorie looked as if her cup of bliss were full and running over.

"And after that," said Mrs. Maynard, "if none of you object too seriously, we thought perhaps a little run up through New England would prove attractive."

"Mother," said King, looking at her twinkling eyes, "you planned all this out before? It's no surprise to you!"

"Very true, King; your father and I planned it while we were on our Southern trip. We had such a delightful outing, it seemed only fair that we should take you children for a trip also. And your father has been thinking for some time about buying an automobile, and as he can take the time now, it all works in beautifully."

"Beautiful! I should think it was!" cried Marjorie; "and Mother, will we all have motor coats and goggles, and all those queer things that they wear in automobiles?"

"You won't have any queer things, and I doubt if you'll need goggles; but you and Kitty shall have pretty motor coats, and pretty hoods and veils. We'll go on Monday to buy them."

"Oh," sighed Marjorie, "it just does seem too good to be true! It's like a fairy dream, and I 'spect I'll wake up every minute. What about lessons, Mother?"

"We've thought of that; but as your lessons would stop the first of June anyway, you'll only lose a few weeks, and so we're going to take you all out of school for that time. For this year, at any rate, Maytime shall be playtime for the Maynards."

"I'm so glad I'm a Maynard, and live in the Maynard family," said Kitty, with a deep sigh of satisfaction.

"So'm I," declared Marjorie; "there never was such a nice family, with such a bee-yootiful father and mother!"

And as if this were a signal for a general onslaught, the three young Maynards made a dash for the two older Maynards, and nearly choked them with well-meant but rather athletic embraces, which was their fashion of expressing approval and appreciation.

CHAPTER III
A TRIAL TRIP
Owing to some unexpected delay, the automobile didn't arrive until
Wednesday. But when at last it came whirring up the drive, the assembled
Maynards on the veranda greeted it with shouts of approval.
"Did you ever see such a beauty!" cried Marjorie, as she danced around the new car, and clambering up on the farther side, jumped over the closed door, and fell plump into one of the cushioned seats.

"Oh, Mopsy!" cried her father, "that isn't the way to get in."

"I don't care,—I am in! And it's just great in here! Why, there's room enough for a whole party."

The chauffeur who brought the car seemed a little surprised at the antics of the children, for he was a stolid Englishman, and not much accustomed to American exuberance.

Mr. Maynard had engaged him on the best recommendations, and felt sure that he was a trust-worthy and capable man. His name was Pompton, and he was large and muscular, with a face that was grave but not ill-natured.

Kingdon made friends with him at once, and climbing up into the seat beside him, asked innumerable questions about the various parts of the machine.

"Suppose we go at once for a trial spin," proposed Mr. Maynard, and almost before he had completed his sentence, a chorus of assent rose in response.

"Oh, do, Father," cried King; "and let me stay here in front, so I can see how it works."

"Some other time you may do that, King, but this time I want to sit in front myself, so hop out, and take one of the orchestra chairs."

"All right, sir," and King tumbled out, and flew around to the other side of the car. Mrs. Maynard, Kitty, and Rosamond were already seated in the wide, comfortable back seat. This left two seats in the tonneau for King and Marjorie, and with Mr. Maynard in front, by the side of Pompton, the car offered perfect accommodations for the Maynard family. It was a big touring car of a most approved make, and up-to-date finish. The top could be opened or closed at will, and there were many appurtenances and clever contrivances for comfort, designed to add to the delights of a long tour.

The family had been so eager to start at once that they had not paused to get hats or wraps, and as the top was down, the strong breeze blew their hair all about, and also made conversation a little difficult.

But the Maynard children were not baffled by difficulties, and they raised their voices until they were audible in spite of the wind.

"Isn't it magnificent!" screamed Marjorie, pulling at King's collar to attract his attention.

"Perfectly gorgiferous!—and then some!" he yelled back, a little preoccupied in manner, because he was leaning over the chauffeur's shoulder, in his impatience to learn how to run the machine.

They went flying through the streets of Rockwell, and out into the country for a little run. Then as they were to start on their tour next day, Mrs. Maynard declared they must be turning homeward.

"Oh, Father," cried Marjorie, "after Mother gets out, mayn't we take
Delight out for a few moments? Even only just around the block?"
"Will she care to go, Mopsy? You know an automobile isn't such a wonderful novelty to her as it is to you."

"Oh, yes, she'll care to go in ours,—and anyway I mean just for a minute."

13

"All right then, chickabiddy; we'll put Mother and Baby out, then we'll take Delight around the block, and that'll be about all for to-day."

So Mrs. Maynard and Rosy Posy were deposited on their own doorstep, and the big red car flew across the street to give Delight an exhibition of its glories.

She was glad to go, but she was far from being as enthusiastic as the Maynard children, for Delight was a timid little girl, and never felt entirely at her ease in a fast-flying motor. She nestled in the back seat between Marjorie and Kitty, and grasped both their hands when the car swung swiftly around a corner.

Then they happened to meet Flip Henderson walking along the street, and they picked him up as an extra passenger, and then Kitty said: "Oh, now we've got the whole Jinks Club except Dorothy Adams. Do let's stop for her, Father, and then go round one more block."

Good-natured Mr. Maynard consented, and though there was no vacant seat, Dorothy was bundled in somehow, and the crowd of shouting, laughing children were driven around several blocks.

The quiet little town of Rockwell was amazed at the sight, and thought it must be some new kind of a circus advertisement, until they realized that it was the Maynard family, and people had long ceased to be surprised at what the Maynards did.

But at last the children who were not Maynards were left at their respective homes, and the big red car again turned in at its own home.

"Where are you going to keep it, Father?" asked King, as they all scrambled out.

"I shall have a garage built on the place as soon as we get back; but for to-night our pet will have to sleep in other lodgings. Skip into the house now, you children, for I want to talk to Pompton without the interruption of a crowd of chatter-boxes."

So the three went into the house and stood together at a front window, flattening their noses against the glass, as they looked out at their new treasure. King was in the middle, behind his two sisters, with an arm around both their necks, and he explained to them in a very learned way, a great many points about the machine that they did not understand. His explanations were far from being correct or true, but as he didn't know that, nor the girls either, it really made no difference.

At last Pompton drove away with the car, and they watched it disappear down the street, and then turned to greet Mr. Maynard as he entered.

Marjorie went straight up to her father, and stood in front of him.

"I do think you are the most wonderful Father in the whole world," she said, eyeing him in a judicial manner.

"And the grandest!" said Kitty, snuggling herself in under his arm.

14

"And the tip-toppest!" declared King, grasping his father's other hand.

"Well, well!" exclaimed Mr. Maynard, dropping into an armchair, "I am certainly catching some fine compliments! And I'd like to return them. I don't mind confessing that I think you young people just about the highest class of goods in the market!"

"But we're not as splendid as you are," said Marjorie, thoughtfully; "because you do things for us, and we never do anything for you."

"Oh, yes, you do," returned her father; "you do all I want you to, by just living, and growing, and trying to behave yourselves properly."

"But we don't always do that," said Kitty, with a repentant air.

"You do, Kit," said King, generously, "you're always good. Mops and I are the ones that slip up."

"It's human nature to slip up occasionally," said Mr. Maynard, "but I think on the whole my kiddies do pretty well. Now, as you know, we start to-morrow for Grandma Sherwood's, and while I'm not going to give you a lecture on the subject, I am going to ask you to behave pretty fairly well while you're at her house. You know she's not as young as she once was, and a lot of mischievous children may make her a great deal of trouble if they wish to,—or they can refrain from doing so. Need I say any more?"

"Not another word, Father," declared Marjorie; "I promise to be as good as pie,—custard pie!"

"And I'll be as good as mince pie," said King, "you can't beat that!"

"Yes, I can," said Kitty; "I shall be as good as lemon meringue pie,—with a high, fluffy meringue, and little browny wiggles all over the top."

"You've struck it, Kit," said her brother, admiringly; "that is the best kind of pie,—and you'll be the best of the Maynard bunch! Say, Kitty, doesn't it hurt you to be so good?"

"No," said Kitty, placidly, "I like it."

There was not much fun in teasing Kitty, she was too matter-of-fact, so King turned his attentions to Marjorie, and with apparent innocence kicked out his foot just in time for her to stumble over it. This led to a general scrimmage, in which two Maynards, two sofa-pillows, and a footstool became very much tangled up, and Mr. Maynard and Kitty sat smiling indulgently at them, with the air of enjoying the performance and not caring to take part in it.

Of course the dinner hour and all the hours until bedtime were occupied in conversation about the projected trip, and when at last the little Maynards were tucked into bed, their dreams still continued to hover around the same subject.

* * * * *

The next day proved to be most kindly disposed as to weather, and the brilliant May sunshine sparkled on the big red car as it stood waiting for its passengers.

There was more or less hurry and scurry of getting ready, but the elder Maynards were of systematic and methodical habits, so that really everything was ready ahead of time. Two trunks had been sent on by express to Grandma Sherwood's, and one large trunk which was to accompany them on their trip, was already fastened in place at the back of the car.

The children all had new motor coats of pongee, which they could wear over other wraps if necessary. The girls also had fascinating little hoods of shirred silk, Marjorie's being rose color, and Kitty's blue. They greatly admired themselves and each other in these costumes, and Marjorie declared it gave her a trippy feeling just to look at them.

They started at ten o'clock. Mrs. Maynard and Kitty sat back with
Rosamond between them. Midget and King in the next two seats, and Mr.
Maynard in front with the chauffeur.
They went flying down the drive to a chorus of good-byes from the servants, who assembled to see them off, and who would take care of the house in their absence.

As they whizzed across the street, and paused for a moment in front of Delight's house, Delight and Miss Hart came running down to wave a good-bye, and their hands were full of flowers which they flung into the automobile all over its merry occupants.

"Good-bye, good-bye!" they called, for the Maynards had not stopped, but merely slowed down a little, and were now again speeding on their way. Marjorie and King stood up in their places, and waved handkerchiefs and flowers, and shouted good-bye until they could no longer be seen or heard.

"Now we are really started," said Marjorie, settling back into her seat with an air of great satisfaction. "Having all these flowers thrown at us seems like a wedding trip or something. There's not nearly so much wind to-day, and then, with this hood, my hair doesn't blow about so, anyway. Oh, Father, I'm awful hungry! Can't we stop at the grocer's and get some ginger-snaps and apples?"

"You've just had your breakfast, but I suppose automobile kiddies must have something to nibble on!" So a stop was made at the grocer's, and a supply of ginger-snaps and apples was added to their other luggage.

Mr. Hiller, the grocer, was very much interested in the motor party, and came out himself to wish them good speed.

"I don't know what Rockwell will do without the Maynard tribe," he said; "you youngsters keep things lively around town. And you're going to be away a month, you say. Well, well!"

"Perhaps it's a good thing to give the town a little rest, Mr. Hiller," said Mr. Maynard, laughing.

"No, sir; no, sir; them children of yours never does anything vicious. Full of mischief they may be, full of fun they may be, but never really naughty. No, no!"

Mr. Maynard expressed a laughing appreciation of these compliments, and then they started once more.

"Now we're really off," said King, "we won't have to stop again."

"Oh, I think most of the fun is stopping," said Marjorie; "I love to stop and then go on again. Perhaps we can get out and pick some wild flowers or wade in a brook."

"Not to-day," said her father, "but some days you may do that to your heart's content. The whole trip is going to be just one long picnic, and we're going to get all the fun out of it we possibly can."

"I think it's delicious," said Kitty, in her quiet way; "I think it's fun enough just to glide along like this, with the blue sky shining all over us, and the trees waving their boughs at us, and even the fences jig-jigging along at our side."

"You're so poetical, Kitty," said Marjorie; "I love the blue sky and the green trees too, but just now I want to see a red apple and a brown ginger-snap!"

"Midget, I believe you could eat at any time," said her mother, laughing.

"Yes, I could," said Midget, contentedly, "'cept when I've just had enough. And I do feel like eating, but I feel like singing, too."

"You can't do both at once," said her brother.

"No, but I can do first one and then the other. Now I'll tell you, Father, what to do. You make a little song for us, while I eat this apple. A kind of a little motor song, you know."

So while Marjorie ate her apple, and the other children engaged in the same pursuit, Mr. Maynard made a little song for them.

This was a favorite game of the Maynards. Father Maynard had a knack of turning off verses, and they usually sang them to some well-known air, or perhaps made up a little crooning tune of their own.

So when the apples were finished and the cores flung away, Mr. Maynard lined out his little song, and the children quickly learned it.

After two or three attempts they were able to sing it correctly, and they stowed it away in their memory as one of their favorite songs, and at intervals throughout the day their young voices filled the air with these sentiments:

"Very happy the Maynards are;

17

Taking a tour in their motor car
Gaily to Grandma's lickety-split
Marjorie, Rosamond, Kingdon, and Kit
Mothery, fathery, also along,—
Gaily we sing our motor car song!
   Hooray, hooray!
   For our holiday
May for the Maynards!
   Maynards for May!"

CHAPTER IV

VISITING A CAMP

Rockwell was soon left far behind, and the Maynards' car flew along the country road, now passing through a bit of woods, and now through a little town, or again crossing a picturesque brook.

The children were delighted with the new experience, and chatted all at once, about the roadside sights.

Pompton, the English chauffeur, though he said little or nothing, was secretly amazed at the gaiety and volubility of the young people. The children were allowed to take turns sitting in the front seat, and, as was their nature, they talked rapidly and steadily to the somewhat taciturn driver.

"What a funny name you have, Pompton," said Marjorie, as she sat beside him; "at least it seems funny to me, because I never heard it before."

"It's a good old English name, Miss," he returned, a little gruffly, "and never been dishonored, as I know of."

"Oh, I think it's a very nice name," said Marjorie, quickly, for she had had no intention of being unpleasantly critical, "only I think it's a funny name. You see Pompton sounds so much like pumpkin."

"Do you think so, Miss?"

"Oh, well, it doesn't matter about a name, anyway. Tell me about your people. Have you any little boys and girls?"

"No, Miss; I never was married, Miss. And I ain't overly fond of children."

"Really, aren't you, Pompton? Well, you'll have to begin being fond of them, because you see, us Maynard children just can't stand anybody around who isn't fond of us. Though of course we've never tried, for everybody who has lived with us has always been terribly fond of us."

"Maybe it'll be a pleasant change then, Miss, to try another sort." Pompton's eyes twinkled good-naturedly as he said this, and Marjorie instinctively recognized that he was trying to joke.

"Ah, you're fond of us already, Pompton, and you needn't say you're not! It's a funny thing," she went on, confidentially, "but everybody loves us Maynards,—and yet we're such a bad lot."

"A bad lot, Miss?"

"Well, full of the old scratch, you know; always cutting up jinks. Do you know what jinks are, Pompton?"

"No, Miss; what are they?"

"Why they're just jinks; something to cut up, you know."

"Cut up, Miss?"

"Oh, Pompton, you're just like a parrot! You just repeat what I say!
Don't you know anything?"
"Very little, Miss."

But as they rode along, and Marjorie asked her interminable string of questions about the car, or about the trees or flowers they were passing, or about sundry roadside matters, she found that Pompton was a very well-informed man, indeed, as well as being kind and obliging in answering questions.

As they spun along a bit of straight road, Marjorie saw, some distance ahead, a girl sitting on a large stone by the roadside. The girl's face was so weary and pained-looking that Marjorie felt a sudden thrill of pity for her, and as a second glance showed that the girl was lame, she impulsively begged Pompton to stop a moment that they might speak to her.

The chauffeur turned around to see if the order were corroborated by the older people, and Mrs. Maynard said, "Yes, Pompton, let us stop and see what the poor girl wants."

So the car stopped, and Marjorie impetuously jumped out, and ran to speak to the girl, who seemed ill and suffering. Mr. Maynard joined them at once, and they listened to the girl's story.

She said her name was Minnie Meyer, and that she had to walk to the neighboring town to buy some provisions for her mother. But being lame she had become so tired that she sat down to rest by the way.

"How far have you to go, child?" asked Mr. Maynard, kindly.

"I have already walked a mile, sir, and it's two miles more to Pelton, where I must go. I have often walked the distance, but my foot is very bad just now, and it is hard going. I have been ill, and I am not yet very strong."

19

"I should think not!" exclaimed King, who had jumped out to see what was going on. "Look here, Father, we're going directly to Pelton; it is a straight road, and I can't miss the way. You let this girl take my place in the car, and I'll walk."

"Now that's good of you, King," said his father with an approving glance at the boy, "for this poor child is pretty well tired out. How can you get home again, Minnie?"

"Oh, sir, I shall have a ride home. A neighbor of ours will take me; but I have to walk over to Pelton and get my things by the time he's ready to start."

"And what time does he start for home?"

"About two o'clock, sir."

The child's face was very white, and her eyes were large and dark. Though probably no older than Marjorie, she looked careworn and troubled beyond her years.

"You are a good boy, King," his mother called out from the car, "and I think, Ed, we had better take the girl with us. Kingdon won't mind a two miles' walk, I know, when it is in such a good cause."

"I'm going with King," announced Marjorie; "I shan't mind the walk, either, and it will be fun for both of us to be together, while it would be awful lonesome for King all alone."

"Good for you, Mopsy Midget!" cried King, "you're a trump! Come on, we'll get there before the car does." King grasped his sister's hand, and they set off merrily at a good pace along the straight road to Pelton.

Meantime, Mr. Maynard had assisted the lame girl into the car, and Kitty tucked rugs and shawls around her to make her comfortable.

Minnie Meyer was both awestruck and delighted. She had never been in an automobile before, and it had all happened so quickly she scarcely realized her good fortune.

"I think you must all be angels," she said; "and I'm sorry the young lady and gentleman have to walk so far, and all just for me."

"But they're better able to walk than you are," said practical Kitty.

"That may be, Miss, but it seems queer for the likes of me to be riding in their place. My! But it goes fast!"

The car passed King and Marjorie, who waved their hands gaily, and watched it rapidly disappear along the road in front of them.

"I'm glad we're doing a deed of charity, Midget," said her brother, "for if we weren't I shouldn't relish this long walk very much."

"Now, King, don't go and spoil your noble deed by growling about it! It was lovely of you to let that girl ride in your place, but if you're going to kick about walking, you'll spoil it all."

"I'm not kicking. And anyway, Mops, you were the noble one yourself. You walked just so I shouldn't be lonesome."

"'Course I did! What's lots of fun for two is awful poky for one. Come on, I'll race you to that big sticking-out tree!"

They flew along the road with their heels kicking out behind, and though King reached the tree first, he was only a few steps ahead of Marjorie, who came up panting, and threw herself on the grass by his side.

"We mustn't do that again," she said, "it makes us too much out of breath, and we can't walk afterward. Now let's rest a minute, and then walk on just middling fast,—because it's a long way yet. What time do you suppose we'll get there?"

"Pomp said if we'd walk straight along we ought to get to the inn by half-past twelve. They won't have lunch till we get there."

"You bet they won't! Do you know where the inn is?"

"Well, I've never been there, but when we get to Pelton I rather guess we can find the inn! Come on, Mops, if you're rested, we'd better get a move on!"

Then they trudged on together, finding the way very pleasant, and many things to interest them as they passed along.

The road was a public highway, and there were many motor cars and much other traffic.

But as the children kept on a grassy path by the side of the road they were in no danger, and there was no possibility of losing their way.

"It's just a matter of keeping at it," said King, "but it does seem longer than I thought. We're not halfway yet."

"How do you know?"

"'Cause Pomp said when we came to the sign-board pointing to Mossville we'd be halfway, and we haven't come to that yet."

"What makes you call him Pomp?"

"Oh, just for short; and besides he's kind of pompous, you know,—sort of stuffy and English."

"Yes, he is. I like him, though, and I think he's going to like us, but he doesn't understand us yet. I hope Father will ask that lame girl to lunch with us. I think she looked hungry."

"She looked awful poor, and I s'pose poor folks are always hungry. It must be awful to be always hungry, Mops!"

"Well, I'm 'most always hungry myself."

"Oh, that isn't real hunger; that's just wanting something to eat. Hello, here's the Mossville sign now! See it?"

"Yes; so now we must be halfway. I'm not tired, are you?"

"No, not a bit. I'd like a drink of water, though. Perhaps we'll come to a brook."

But they walked on considerably further without seeing any brook, or even a farmhouse where they might stop for a drink of water. But when they were about half a mile from Pelton, King saw a little bridge off toward the right, and exclaimed, "That bridge must be over water of some sort. If you want to, Midget, we can go over and see if it's clean enough to drink."

"Come on, then; it won't take long, and I'm 'most choked to death."

They walked across an intervening field, and came to the little bridge which did cross a small but clear and sparkling brook.

"What can we drink out of?" asked Midget.

"Have to drink out of our hands, I guess; wish we had a cup or something.
Oh, look at that man!"
Midget looked in the direction King pointed, and saw a man seated on the ground, busily working at something which seemed to be made of long rushes of reeds.

"He's making a basket," cried King, greatly interested. "Let's go and look at him."

They trotted over to the man, and King said, politely, "Is that a basket you're making, sir?"

"Yes," came the answer in a gruff voice, and when the man looked up at them, they saw he was a strange-looking person indeed. His complexion was dark, his coarse black hair rather long, and his black eyes had a shrewd expression, but were without kindliness. "What do you want?" he said, still in his gruff voice.

"We don't want anything p'ticular," said Marjorie, who did not wish to be intrusive; "we did want a drink of water out of the brook, but we had nothing to drink from, and then we saw you building a basket, and we just came over to look at you. You don't mind, do you?"

"No, I don't mind," and the man's voice was a little less gruff as he looked at Marjorie's pretty smiling face. Then he gave her another look, somewhat more scrutinizing, and then he looked again at King. "You want a drink of water, do you?" and the look of interest in his round black eyes seemed to become intensified. "Well, I'll tell you what to do; you go right straight

22

along that little path through the grass, and after a few steps, you'll find some people, and they'll give you a drink of water with pleasure, and a nice cup to drink it out of."

"Is it far?" asked Marjorie, for she couldn't see any signs of habitation, and did not wish to delay too long.

"No; 'tain't a dozen steps. Just behind that clump of trees yonder; you can't miss it."

"A farmhouse, I suppose," said King.

"Well, not just exactly a farmhouse," said the man, "but you go on, you youngsters, and whoever you see when you get there, tell 'em Jim sent you."

"We will; and thank you, Jim," said Marjorie, suddenly remembering her manners.

"You're welcome," said the man, and again his voice was gruff as at first.

"Somehow I don't like it, Mops," said King, who had a troubled look on his face as they walked swiftly along the path indicated.

"Don't like what?"

"His sending us over here. And I don't like him; he didn't look right."

"I thought he was very kind to tell us about the farmhouse, and if his voice is sort of gruff, I s'pose he can't help that."

"It isn't that exactly; but I think he's a,—a—"

"A what?"

"Never mind; here we are at the place. Why, Mops, it isn't a house at all! It's a tent,—a lot of tents."

"So it is! It must be an encampment. Do you think there are soldiers here?"

"Soldiers? No! I only wish they were soldiers."

As King was speaking, a young woman came walking toward them, smiling in an ingratiating way. Like the man, Jim, she was dark-haired and dark-skinned. Her black eyes flashed, and her smiling red lips showed very white teeth as she spoke kindly to the children.

"Come in," she said, in a wheedling voice; "come in; I love little boys and girls. What do you want?"

Marjorie began to say, "We want a drink of water," when King pinched her elbow as a sign to be quiet, and he spoke to the woman himself. "We don't want anything," he said, "we're just passing by on our way to Pelton. Good-morning."

23

Grasping Marjorie's arm he turned to go away, but the woman stopped him, saying, "Oh, don't go so quickly; come in and rest a moment, and I will give you a drink of milk, and then you can go on to Pelton."

"Yes, let's do that, King," said Marjorie, looking at her brother, amazed at his ungracious actions.

But King persisted in his determination. "No, thank you," he said to the woman in a decided way; "you're very kind, but we don't care for any milk, and we must go right on to Pelton."

"And I say you must stay right here," said the woman, in much sterner tones than she had used before, and taking the children each by an arm, she pushed them ahead of her inside of the largest tent.

CHAPTER V
HELD CAPTIVE

Then King's fears were realized. He had suspected these people were gypsies, and now he discovered that they were. Inside the tent were three or four men and women, all of the dark, gypsy type, and wearing the strange, bright-colored garments characteristic of their tribe. They did not seem ill-disposed toward the visitors, but welcomed them cordially, and one of the women went at once for a pitcher of milk, and brought it, with two glasses, which she set on the table.

King was not exactly frightened, for they all seemed pleasant and kind enough, but he couldn't help remembering how gypsies were credited with the habit of stealing children, and holding them for ransom. "But only babies," he thought to himself; "I don't believe they ever steal such big kids as Marjorie and me."

King was fifteen, and tall for his age, and as he looked at Marjorie he realized that she was a big girl, too, and he felt sure they were beyond the age of being kidnapped. But as he noted the furtive glances which were cast at them by the gypsies, he again felt alarmed, and glanced at Marjorie to see if her thoughts were like his own.

But they were not. Marjorie was chatting gaily with the good-looking young woman who had brought her into the tent, and she was accepting an invitation to have a glass of milk and a cracker.

As an old gypsy woman poured the milk from the pitcher into the glass, she turned her back to Marjorie, but King's alert eyes could see her shaking a small portion of white powder into the milk.

Like a flash it came to King what it all meant! They were kidnappers, these wicked gypsies, and they meant to put some drug in the milk that the children drank, so they would go to sleep, and then the kidnappers would carry them away!

King thought rapidly. He couldn't let Marjorie drink that milk,—and yet if he made a fuss about it, they could easily overpower him. He determined to use strategy.

"Let me pass the glass to my sister," he said, jumping up, and going to take the glass from the old woman who had poured it. Unsuspectingly, she let him take it, but as he turned, he stumbled, purposely, against the table leg, and spilled all the milk on the ground.

"Oh, excuse me," he said, politely. "Now we shall have to go without a drink of milk! But we are just as much obliged, and we bid you good-morning. Come, Midget."

Marjorie was at a loss to understand King's actions, but she knew her brother well enough to know that his tone and his look meant that something very serious was the matter, and she was quite ready to obey him without knowing why.

But though he grasped her arm, and endeavored to lead her out of the tent, they were suddenly stopped. Two stalwart men who had been sitting in shadow at the back of the tent came forward, and grasping the children's shoulders, pushed them back into their seats rather roughly.

"You set down there!" said one of the men, "and don't you move till you're told to! We ain't decided just what to do with you yet, and when we see fit, we'll tell you, and not till then, so you just keep still!"

Marjorie suddenly sensed the situation. These people were enemies, not friends! She understood King's efforts to get her away, and she remembered, too, his misgivings as they were on their way across the field.

Moreover, it was she who had insisted on coming, and so she felt, in a way, responsible for what had happened to them. She jumped to her feet as soon as the man let go of her shoulder, and cried, with flashing eyes, "I will not keep still! What do you mean by treating me like that? Don't you know who I am? We're Maynards! We're Edward Maynard's children,—and everybody loves the Maynards!"

"Oh, they do, do they!" said the man who had spoken before. "Then that's a mighty good reason why we should keep you here a little while."

"Keep us here!" stormed Marjorie, not at all realizing that they were being kidnapped, but merely thinking these people were playing some sort of a joke upon them. "Why should you keep us here? We want to go on."

"You want to go on, do you?" And the man fairly snarled at them; "well, you can't go on, and you may as well understand that! Didn't Jim send you?"

"Yes, Jim sent us," said Marjorie, remembering what the man who was weaving the basket had said.

"Then if Jim sent you, you're here to stay. And as it's just impossible for you to get away, there's small use in your trying! So you may as well make the best of it, and if you don't want your bread and milk you needn't eat it, but if you do, you can have it. There, now, I'm speaking fair by you, and you may as well behave yourselves."

25

"Speaking fair by us!" exclaimed Marjorie, who was as yet more indignant than frightened. "Do you call it speaking fair by us to tell us that we must stay here when we want to go on! You are bad, wicked men!"

"Yes, little Miss," was the answer, with a shout of laughter, "we are bad, wicked men! Now what are you going to do about it? You don't fancy for a minute that you can get away, do you?"

This silenced Marjorie, for there was no answer to such a question. Her rage had spent itself in her impetuous speech, and she knew of course that two children could not get away from this band of villains if they were not allowed to do so. But she did not cry. Her feelings were too wrought up for that. She sat where they had placed her, and tried bravely to conceal the fright and fear that were every moment growing stronger within her. She gave one imploring glance at King, and he came over and sat beside her. He took her hand in a tight clasp, implying that whatever happened they would face it together.

"Keep 'em there for the present," growled the man who seemed to be the spokesman, and then he and the other man went away, leaving the children in care of the three gypsy women.

Although apparently the women paid little attention to their young prisoners, King and Midget could easily see that the eyes of their jailers were ever alert, and watching their slightest movement. Had they tried to cut and run, they would have been caught before they reached the door. But no heed was paid when they whispered together, and so they were able to hold a long conversation which was unheard, and even unnoticed by the others.

"You know, Mops, what has happened?" whispered King.

"No, I don't; what do they want of us?"

"Why, we're kidnapped and held for ransom. Those men have probably gone out now to send letters to Father about the ransom money."

"Oh, then Father'll pay it, and we'll get away."

"It isn't so easy as that. They have lots of fussing back and forth. We may be here a long time. I say, Mops, you're a brick not to cry."

"I'm too mad to cry. The idea of their keeping us here like this! It's outrageous! Why, King, by this time we would have been in Pelton. Just think how worried Father and Mother must be!"

"Don't think about that, Mops, or you will cry sure. And I will, too!
Let's think how to get away."
But thinking was of little use, as there was no way to get away but to run out at the door, and an attempt at that would be such certain failure that it was not worth trying.

26

So the children sat there in dumb misery, silently watching the gypsy women as they moved about preparing the mid-day meal.

Occasionally they spoke, and their manner and words were kindly, but King and Midget could not bring themselves to respond in the same way.

"King," whispered Marjorie, "how far do you suppose we are from the road?"

"Too far to run there, if that's what you mean. We'd be caught before we started," was the whispered reply.

"That isn't what I mean; but how far are we?"

"Not very far, Midget; after we crossed the little bridge, the path to this place was sort of parallel to the road."

"Well, King, I've got an idea. Don't say anything, and don't stop me."

With a stretch and a yawn as of great weariness, Marjorie slowly rose. Immediately the three women started toward her. "You sit still!" said one, sharply.

"Mayn't I walk about the room, if I promise not to go out the door?" said Marjorie; "I'm so cramped sitting still."
"Move around if you want to," said the youngest of the women, a little more gently; "but there's no use your trying to run away," and she wagged her head ominously.

"Honest, I won't try to run away," and Marjorie's big, dark eyes looked gravely at her captor.

The women said nothing more, and Marjorie wandered about the tent in an apparently aimless manner. But after a time she came near to a small slit in the side of the tent that served as a sort of window, and here she paused and examined some beads that hung near by. Then choosing a moment when the women were most attentive to their household duties, she put her head out through the window and yelled. Now Marjorie Maynard's yell was something that a Comanche Indian might be proud of. Blessed with strong, healthy lungs, and being by nature fond of shouting, she possessed an ability to scream which was really unusual.

As her blood-curdling shouts rent the air, the three women were so stupefied that for a moment they could say or do nothing. This gave Marjorie additional time, and she made the most of it. Her entire lung power spent itself in successive shrieks more than a dozen times, before she was finally dragged away from the window by the infuriated gypsy women.

Marjorie turned upon them, unafraid.

"I told you I wouldn't try to run away," she said, "and neither I didn't. But I had a right to yell, and if anybody heard me, I hope he'll come right straight here! You are bad, wicked women!"

The child's righteous indignation had its effect on the women, and they hesitated, not knowing exactly what to do with this little termagant.

And strange to say, Marjorie's ruse had succeeded.

For when the Maynards reached Pelton, and had found the inn where they were to lunch, Pompton, the chauffeur, had expressed himself as unwilling to sit there quietly and await the arrival of King and Marjorie.

"The poor children will be done out," he said to Mr. Maynard, "and by your leave, sir, I'll just take the car, and run back a few rods and pick them up."

"That's good of you, Pompton," said Mr. Maynard, appreciatively. "They can't be far away now, but they'll be glad of a lift."

So Pompton turned the car about, and started back along the road he had just come. To his surprise, he did not meet the children as soon as he had expected, and as he continued his route without seeing them, he began to be really alarmed. He passed the halfway sign, and went nearly to the place where he had left them and had taken in the lame girl.

"There's something happened to them," he said to himself. "My word! I knew those children ought not to be left to themselves! They're too full of mischief. Like as not they've trailed off into the woods, and how can I ever find them?"

Wondering what he had better do, Pompton turned the car around, and slowly went back toward Pelton. At every crossroad or side path into the woods he paused and shouted, but heard no response. When at last he came near the place where the children had really turned off toward the brook, he stopped and looked about. Seeing smoke issuing from among the trees at a little distance, he thought, "That's a gypsy camp. Now wouldn't it be just like those youngsters to trail in there? Anyway it's the most likely place, and I'm going to have a look."

Leaving his car by the side of the road, Pompton struck into the field, and soon came to the little bridge just beyond which the old basket-weaver still sat.

"Have you seen anything of two children?" Pompton inquired, civilly.

"No," growled the man, looking up and frowning a little.

"Well, I'm fairly sure they came in here from the road about half an hour ago. Perhaps you didn't notice them. I'll just take a look round." He started in the direction of the camp, but the man called him back.

"I tell you no children have been near here," he said, in a voice slightly less surly. "If they had, they'd have had to cross this bridge, and I couldn't miss seeing them. I've been here two hours."

This seemed conclusive, and Pompton had no reason to think the man was not telling the truth. But he was without doubt a gypsy, and Pompton had small respect for the veracity of the gypsy. He waited a few moments, pretending to be interested in the man's basketry, but really considering whether to insist on going on to the camp hidden in the trees, or whether to believe the man's statement.

And it was at this moment that Marjorie's shrieks rang out.

"Good heavens!" cried Pompton. "What is that?"

The basket-weaver neither heard nor answered him, for the shrieks continued, and Pompton set off at a run in the direction whence they came. He was not quite sure it was Marjorie's voice, but there was certainly somebody in distress, and Pompton was of a valiant nature.

The smoke issuing above the trees was sufficient guide, and his flying steps soon brought him to the encampment. Flinging open, indeed almost tearing down the flapping door of the tent, he strode inside.

"What's the matter here?" he began, but he could get no further, for with a glad cry the two Maynard children flung themselves into his out-stretched arms.

CHAPTER VI
AT GRANDMA SHERWOOD'S

Aside from his threatening face, red with rage, and stormy with indignation, Pompton's terrifying aspect was increased by the chauffeur's costume which he wore. His goggles were pushed up on his brow, but his eyes darted vengeance, and the three gypsy women were completely cowed at the sight of him.

"You shall pay for this outrage!" he exclaimed; "and don't think you will be let down easy! Kidnapping is a crime that is well punished, and your punishment shall be to the full! I shall take these children away now, but don't think you can escape! I will see to that! Where are your men folks?"

Pompton was a large man, more than six feet high, and heavy in proportion, and as he towered above the frightened gypsy women, they could find no words to answer him.

"I'll find them for myself!" he exclaimed, and taking the children by either hand, he hurried them out of the tent.

As Pompton had surmised, the men had run away to the woods, and hidden themselves, for no trace of them could be seen. The old basket-maker, too, had disappeared, and there was nothing to prevent their departure.

"Miss Marjorie, you're a wonder!" Pompton exclaimed, as they crossed the little bridge and made for the road. "Now, how did you think to shout the very lungs out of you like that?"

"It was the only thing to do, Pompton; they wouldn't let us run away, so there was nothing to do but holler. My! but I'm glad you came!"

"Me, too!" cried King. "I felt awful to sit there and not do anything to rescue Mops, but I couldn't think of a thing to do. I never thought of yelling to beat the band!"

"Of course you didn't, King," said Marjorie. "A boy wouldn't do that. And, anyway, you can't screech like I can."
"I didn't suppose anybody could, Miss Marjorie; I'm sure such screams were never heard before, outside of Bedlam!"

"Well, we're safe now, anyway," cried Marjorie, skipping along gaily by Pompton's side; "and here's our dear, blessed car! Oh, King, I'm so glad we're safe!"

In a reaction of joy, Marjorie threw her arms around her brother's neck, and the tears came to her eyes.

"There, there, Mops," and King patted her shoulders, while there was a suggestion of emotion in his own voice; "it's all right now! Hop in, old girl!"

"Yes, hop in, both of you," said Pompton, "and I'll get you back to Pelton pretty quick, and then I'll set somebody on the track of those villains. They'll not get away!"

The trip to Pelton took but a short time, for Pompton drove as fast as the law allowed. But even so, they found a very much alarmed group waiting for them on the veranda of the little inn.

"Where have you been?" exclaimed Mrs. Maynard, as Marjorie flung her arms around her mother's neck, and burst into violent sobs. The realization that she was safe brought a nervous reaction, and though she had been plucky and brave in the hour of danger, she now collapsed with emotion.

"I'll tell you all about it," said King, grasping his father's hands.
"Midget was the bravest, pluckiest girl, and she saved both our lives."
"What!" cried Mr. Maynard, "have you been in danger?"

Marjorie stopped her sobs a moment, and lifted her head from her mother's shoulder.

"It was P-Pompton saved us! I didn't do any saving,—I only s-screeched!"

"And you screeched good and plenty, Miss Marjorie," said the chauffeur, "which was what saved the day; and, Mr. Maynard, by your leave, I'll take the car a minute, to see if there's anybody in authority in this village. I've a matter to put in their hands."

Without waiting for further explanation, Pompton whizzed away in the big car to find the public officials, and set them on trail of the gypsies. For though unsuccessful, their base attempt at kidnapping ought not to go unpunished.

Kingdon told a straightforward story of all that had happened. Unlike Marjorie, he was not overcome by emotion, and though somewhat excited after the experience they had had, he gave a clear and direct account of it all.

Mrs. Maynard held Marjorie closer as she heard of the danger they had been in, and Mr. Maynard laid his hand on the shoulder of his tall son, and heartily exonerated him from all blame in the matter.

"I suppose," King said, a little dubiously, "we ought not to have gone on to the camp; but Mops,—I mean, we were both thirsty,—and we thought it was a farmhouse."

"Of course you did," said Mrs. Maynard; "you did nothing wrong whatever."

"I did," said Midget, penitently; "after we passed the horrid basket-man, King sort of thought he was a gypsy, and he thought we'd better turn back, but I insisted on going on."

"Nothing of the sort!" exclaimed King. "Mops isn't a bit to blame! I did think maybe the man was a gypsy,—and I ought to have insisted on going back."

"Well, well," said Mr. Maynard, "don't strive so hard for the honor of being to blame. It's all over now, and for the present let's forget it, while we eat our luncheon, because it might interfere with our digestion. We're truly thankful to have you back, and we're going to show our thankfulness by not worrying or lamenting over what might have been."

Mr. Maynard's gaiety, though it was really a little forced, had a good effect on the others. For, had he taken a melancholy attitude, they were quite ready to follow suit.

As it was, they all cheered up, and with bright faces followed Mr. Maynard to the dining-room. Kitty slipped her hand in Marjorie's as they went along. She had said little while the story was being told, but as Marjorie well knew, silence with Kitty was always indicative of deep emotion.

The inn, though modern, was copied after a quaint old plan, and the low-ceiled, raftered dining-room greatly pleased the children. There were seats along the wall—something like church pews,—with long tables in front of them. Mr. Maynard had ordered a dainty and satisfying luncheon, and Marjorie and King soon found that thrilling experiences improve the appetite.

Led by Mr. Maynard, the table talk was gay, light, and entertaining; and though Mrs. Maynard could not quite play up to this key, yet she did her best, and carefully hid the tremors that shook her as she looked at her two older children.

"What became of Minnie Meyer?" asked Marjorie, suddenly, for in the stress of circumstances she had almost forgotten the lame girl.

"I tried my best to persuade her to lunch with us," said Mrs. Maynard, "but she would not do so. She was very shy and timid, and though very glad to have the ride, she was unwilling to let us do more for her. She had many errands to attend to, and she was sure of a ride home, so she said we need not worry about her."

"I'm glad she had the ride," said Marjorie, thoughtfully; "and of course it wasn't her fault that the morning turned out as it did."

"No, it wasn't," said King, "and it wasn't our fault either! It wasn't anybody's fault; it just happened."

"And now it happens that it's all over," said his father, still insistently cheerful, "and the incident is closed, and it's past history, and we've all forgotten it. Have some more chicken, King?"

"Yes," said King, "these forgotten experiences make a fellow terribly hungry!"

The subject of the morning's disaster was not again referred to, and Mr. Maynard triumphantly succeeded in his determination to eliminate all thought of it.

By two o'clock Pompton was at the door with the car, and they started gaily off to continue their journey.

Mr. Maynard sat in front with the chauffeur, and if they indulged in some whispered conversation it was not audible to those in the tonneau.

Midget and King themselves had quite recovered their good spirits, and were ready to enjoy the ride through the country.

They went rather fast, as they had started a bit later than they intended, but not too fast to enjoy the scenery or the interesting scenes on either side.

On they went, through towns and villages, past woods and meadows, and up and down moderately high hills. As they neared Morristown, where Grandma Sherwood lived, the hills were higher and the views more picturesque.

It was not yet dusk when they reached Grandma Sherwood's house, and they found the wide gate hospitably open for them. They swung into the driveway, and in another moment they saw Grandma and Uncle Steve on the veranda, waiting to welcome them.

The impetuous Maynard children tumbled out of the car all at once, and fairly swarmed upon their relatives.

"Which is which?" cried Uncle Steve. "Kitty has grown as big as Marjorie was,—and Marjorie has grown as big as King was,—and King has grown as big as,—as a house!"

"And me growed!" cried Rosamond, not wanting to be left out of the comparison.

"You're the biggest of all!" exclaimed Uncle Steve, catching the baby up and seating her on his shoulder, so she could look down on all the others.

"Yes, me biggest of all," she declared, contentedly, as she wound her fat arms around Uncle Steve's neck; "now me go see schickens!"

"Not just now, Rosy Posy," said her mother, "let's all go in the house and see what we can find there."

Easily diverted, the baby went contentedly with her mother, but the mention of chickens had roused in the other children a desire to see the farmyard pets, and King said: "Come on, Mops and Kit, let's us go and see the chickens; come on, Uncle Steve."

"Eliza first!" cried Marjorie, remembering the old cook's friendliness toward them all; "come on!"

Following Midget's lead, the trio went tearing through the house to the kitchen.

Uncle Steve paused in the library where the others were, and said to his sister, "They're the same Maynard children, Helen, if they are a year older. We enjoyed Marjorie last summer, and I know we'll enjoy Kitty this year,—but how you can live with them all at once I can't understand!"

"It's habit," said Mrs. Maynard, smiling, "you know, Steve, you can get used to 'most anything."

"It seems to agree with you, Helen, at any rate," said Grandma Sherwood, looking at her daughter's pink cheeks and bright eyes.

Meanwhile, the younger Maynards had reached the kitchen, and were dancing round Eliza, with shouts of glee.

"Are you glad to see me again, Eliza?" asked Marjorie, flinging herself into the arms of the stout Irishwoman.

"Glad is it, Miss Midget? Faith, I'm thot glad I kin hardly see ye fer gladness! Ye've grow'd,— but I do say not so much as I expicted! But Masther King, now he's as high as the church shpire! And as fer Miss Kitty,—arrah, but she's the dumplin' darlin'! Stan' out there now, Miss Kitty, an' let me look at yez! Och! but yer the foine gurrul! An' it's ye thot's comin' to spend the summer. My! but the toimes we'll be havin'!"

It was a custom of the Maynards for one of the children to spend each summer at Grandma Sherwood's, and as Marjorie had been there last year, it was now Kitty's turn.

"Yes, I'm coming, Eliza," she said, in her sedate way, "but I'm not going to stay now, you know; we're all going on a tour. But I'll come back here the first of June, and stay a long time."

"Any cookies, Eliza?" asked King, apropos of nothing.

"Cookies, is it? There do be, indade! But if yez be afther eatin' thim now, ye'll shpoil yer supper,—thot ye will! Here's one a piece to ye, and now run away, and lave me do me worruk. Be off with yez!"

After accepting a cookie apiece, the children bounced out the back door and down into the garden in search of Carter.

"We've come, Carter; we've come!" cried Marjorie, flinging open a door of the green-house in which Carter was busy potting some plants.

"You don't say so, Miss Mischief! Well, I'm right down glad to see you! And is this Master King? And Miss Kitty? Well, you all grow like weeds after a rain, but I'll warrant you're as full of mischief as ever!"

"Kitty isn't mischievous," said Marjorie, who was proud of the sedate member of the family.

"And it's Miss Kitty who's to spend the summer, isn't it? Well, then, I won't have the times I had last year, pulling children up from down the well,—and picking them up with broken ankles after they slid down the roof! Nothing of that sort, eh?" Carter's eyes twinkled as he looked at Marjorie, who burst into laughter at reminiscences.

"No, nothing of that sort, Carter; but we're all going to be here for a few days, and we're going to give you the time of your life. Will you take us out rowing in the boat?"

"I'll go along with you to make sure you don't drown yourself; but I think you're getting big enough to do your own rowing. I'm not as young as I was, Miss Midget, and I'm chock-full of rheumatism."

"Oh, we'd just as lieve row, Carter; King's fine at it, and I can row pretty well myself."

But Kitty said: "I'm sorry you have rheumatism, Carter; I'll ask Mother to give you something for it."

"Now that's kind and thoughtful of you, Miss Kitty. Miss Mischief, here, would never think of that!" But, as Carter spoke, his eyes rested lovingly on Marjorie's merry face.

"That's so, Carter," she said, a little penitently, "but do you know, I think if you did take us rowing, it would limber up your arms so you wouldn't have rheumatism!"

"Maybe that's so, Miss Mischief,—maybe that's so. Anyway, I'll try both plans, and perhaps it'll help some. But I hear Eliza calling you, so you'd all better skip back to the house. It's nearly supper time."

With a series of wild whoops, which were supposed to be indicative of the general joy of living, the three Maynards joined hands, with Kitty in the middle, and raced madly back to the house.

They all tried to squeeze through the back door at once, which proceeding resulted in an athletic scrimmage, and a final burst of kicking humanity into Eliza's kitchen.

"Howly saints! but ye're the noisy bunch!" was Eliza's greeting, and then she bade them hurry upstairs and tidy themselves for supper.

CHAPTER VII
AN EARLY ESCAPADE
Marjorie and Kitty occupied the room that had been Marjorie's the summer before. Another little white bed had been put up, and as the room was large, the girls were in no way crowded.

Kitty admired the beautiful room, but in her quiet way, by no means making such demonstrations of delight as Marjorie had when she first saw it. Also Kitty felt a sort of possession, as she would return later and occupy the room for the whole summer.

"Lots of these things on the shelf, Midget, I shall have taken away," she said, as the girls were preparing for bed that same night; "for they're your things, and I don't care about them, and I want to make room for my own."

"All right, Kit, but don't bother about them now. When you come back in June, put them all in a big box and have them put up in the attic until I come again. I only hope you'll have as good a time here as I had last summer. Molly Moss and Stella Martin are nearer my age than yours, but you'll like them, I know."

"Oh, I know Molly, but I don't remember Stella."

"You'll prob'ly like Stella best, though, 'cause she's so quiet and sensible like you. Molly's a scalawag, like me."

"All right," said Kitty, sleepily, for she was too tired to discuss the neighbors, and very soon the two girls were sound asleep.

It was very early when Marjorie awoke the next morning. Indeed, the sun had not yet risen, but the coming of this event had cast rosy shadows before. The east was cloudily bright, where the golden beams were trying to break through the lingering shades of night, and the scattering clouds were masses of pink and silver.

When Marjorie opened her eyes, she was so very wide awake that she knew she should not go to sleep again, and indeed had no desire to. The days at Grandma's would be few and short enough anyway, and she meant to improve every shining minute of them, and so concluded to begin before the minutes had really begun to shine.

She hopped out of bed, and, not to wake Kitty, went very softly to the window, and looked out. Across the two wide lawns she could see dimly the outlines of Stella's house, half-hidden by trees, and beyond that she could see the chimneys and gables of Molly's house. She watched the sun poking the tip edge of his circumference above a distant hill, and the bright rays that darted toward her made her eyes dance with sympathetic joy.

"Kitty," she whispered, not wanting to wake her sister, yet wishing she had somebody to share with her the effect of the beautiful sunrise.

"You needn't speak so softly, I'm wide awake," responded Kitty, in her matter-of-fact way; "what do you want?"

"I want you, you goosey! Hop out of bed, and come and see this gorgiferous sunrise!"

Slowly and carefully, as she did everything, Kitty folded back the bedcovers, drew on a pair of bedroom slippers, and then put on a kimona over her frilled nightgown, adjusting it in place and tying its blue ribbon.

"Gracious, Kit! What an old fuss you are! The sun will be up and over and setting before you get here!"

"I'd just as lieve see a sunset as a sunrise, anyway," declared Kitty, as she walked leisurely across the room, just in time to see the great red gold disc tear its lower edge loose from the hill with what seemed almost to be a leap up in the air.

But once at the window, she was as enthusiastic in her enjoyment of the breaking day as Marjorie, though not quite so demonstrative.

"Put on a kimona, Midget," she said at last; "you'll catch cold flying around in your night dress."

"Kit," said her sister, unheeding the admonition, and sitting down on the edge of her bed as she talked, "I've the most splendiferous plan!"

"So've I," said Kitty; "mine is to go back to bed and sleep till breakfast time."

"Pooh! you old Armadillo! Mine's nothing like that."

"Why am I an Armadillo?" asked Kitty, greatly interested to know.

"Because you want to sleep so much."

"That isn't an Armadillo, that's an Anaconda."

"Well, you're it anyway; and it ought to be Armadillo, because it rhymes with pillow! But now, you just listen to my plan. Seem's if I just couldn't wait any longer to see Molly and Stella, and I'm going to dress right, straight, bang, quick! and go over there. Come on."

"They won't be awake."

"Of course they won't; that's the fun of it! We'll throw little pebbles up at their windows, and wake them up, and make them come out."

"Well, all right, I will." Kitty reached this decision after a few moments' consideration, as Marjorie felt sure she would. Kitty usually agreed to her older sister's plans, but she made up her mind slowly, while Midget always reached her conclusions with a hop, skip, and jump.

So the girls began to dress, and in a very few minutes they were buttoning each other's frocks and tying each other's hair ribbons.

Marjorie had invented a way by which they could tie each other's hair ribbons at the same time, but as it oftenest resulted in pulled hair and badly made bows, it was not much of a time-saver after all.

"But I do think, Kit," she said, "being in such haste this morning, we might manage to button each other's dresses at the same time. Stand back to back and let's try."

The trial was a decided failure, and resulted only in a frolic, after which the buttoning was done separately and successfully.

"And anyway, we're not in such a hurry," commented Kitty, "and don't ever try that stunt again, Mopsy. My arms are nearly twisted off!"

"All right, Kit, I won't. Now are you ready? Come on; don't make any noise; we don't want to wake anybody."

They tiptoed downstairs, and as a greater precaution against waking the sleeping grownups, they went through the kitchen, and out at the back door, which they easily unbolted from the inside.

"We'll have to leave this door unfastened," said Marjorie. "I hope no burglars will get in."

"Of course they won't; burglars never come around after sunrise. Oh, isn't it lovely to smell the fresh morningness!"

Kitty stood still, and sniffed the clear, crisp air, while the exhilarating effects of the atmosphere caused Marjorie to dance and prance in circles round her quieter sister.

"When you've sniffed enough, come on, Kit," she said, dancing away toward Stella's house.
Kitty came on, and soon they stood on the greensward directly beneath Stella's bedroom window.
The morning was very still, and the Martins' house looked forbidding, with its silent, closed-up air. It was not yet half-past five, and not even the servants were stirring.

Marjorie's courage failed her. "I guess we won't try Stella first," she whispered to Kitty. "Stella's so scary. Once I just said 'boo' at her, and she cried like fury. If we fire pebbles at her window, like as not she'll think it's a burglar and have yelling hysterics."

"Burglars don't throw pebbles to wake people up."

"Well, Stella's just as likely to think they do. You never can tell what Stella's going to think, or what she's going to do, either. Anyway, let's go to Molly's first; you can't scare her."

"All right," agreed Kitty, and hand in hand the two girls trudged on to the next house.

"I believe I'll get up every morning at five o'clock," said Marjorie; "it is so fresh and green and wet."

"Yes, it's awful wet," said Kitty, looking at her shoes; "but it's a delicious kind of a wetness. Dew is awful different from rain."

"Yes, isn't it; dew makes you think of fairies and,—"

"And spiders," said Kitty, kicking at one of the spider webs with which the grass was dotted.

"Well, I think spiders are sort of fairies," said Marjorie, looking lovingly at the glistening webs; "They must be to weave such silky, spangly stuff."

"They weave it for the fairies, Mops. They weave it in the night; and then about sunrise, the fairies come and gather up the silky, spangly stuff, and take it away to make their dresses out of it. See, they're most all gone now."

"Pooh! the sun dried them up."

"No, he didn't; the fairies came and took them away. Of course you can't see the fairies, and that's why people think the sun dries up the webs." Kitty spoke as one with authority, and into her eyes came the faraway look that always appeared when her imagination was running riot. For a really practical child, Kitty had a great deal of imagination, but the two traits never conflicted.

"This is Molly's window," said Marjorie, dismissing the question of fairies as they reached Mr. Moss's house.

"Why don't you whistle or call her?" suggested Kitty.

"No, that might wake up her father and mother. And besides, throwing pebbles is lots more fun. Let's get a handful from the drive. Get both hands full."

In a moment four little hands were filled with pebbles.

"Wait a minute," said thoughtful Kitty; "let's pick out the biggest ones and throw them away. Some of these big stones might break a window."

So the girls sat down on the front steps and carefully assorted their pebbles until at last they had their hands filled with only the tiniest stones.

"Now the thing is to throw straight," said Marjorie.

"You throw first," said Kitty, "and then I'll follow."

Like a flash, Marjorie's right hand full of pebbles clattered against Molly's window, and was swiftly followed by a second shower from Kitty's right hand. Then they shifted the pebbles in their left hand to their right, and, swish! these pebbles followed the others.

But though the Maynard children were quick, Molly Moss was quicker. At the first pebbles she flew out of bed and flung up the window, raising the sash just in time to get the second lot distributed over her own face and person.

"Oh, Molly, have we hurt you?" called out Kitty, who realized first what they had done.

"No, not a bit! I knew the minute I heard the pebbles it was you girls.
I'm awful glad to see you! Shall I get dressed and come out?"
"Yes, do!" cried Marjorie, who was hopping up and down on one foot in her excitement. "Will it take you long to dress?"

"No, indeed; I'll be down in a jiffy. Just you wait a minute."

It might have been more than a minute, but it wasn't much more, when the girls heard a rustling above them, and looked up to see Molly, fully dressed, climbing out of the window.

"Oh, Molly, you'll break your neck!" cried Kitty, for Molly was already descending by a rose trellis that was amply strong enough for a climbing rose, but which swayed and wabbled frightfully tinder the weight of a climbing girl.

However, Molly didn't weigh very much, and she had the scrambling ability of a cat, so in a few seconds she was down on the ground, and embracing the two Maynard girls both at once.

"You're perfect ducks to come over here so early! How did you get away?"

"Slid out the back door," said Marjorie; "isn't it larky to be around so early in the morning?"

"Perfectly fine! How long are you girls going to stay?"

"Not quite a week, I think," said Kitty, and Marjorie added, "So we want to cram all the fun we can into these few days, and so we thought we'd begin early."

"All right," said Molly, taking her literally, "let's begin right now."

"Oh, we can't do anything now," said Marjorie, "that is, nothing in p'ticular."

"Pooh! yes, we can! It's only about half-past five, and we don't have breakfast till eight, do you?"

"Yes, Grandma has it at eight," said Marjorie, "but, gracious, I'll be starved to death by that time! I'm so hungry now I don't know what to do!"

"I'll tell you what," began Kitty, and upon her face there dawned that rapt expression, which always appeared when she was about to propose something ingenious.

"What?" cried Midget and Molly, both at once.

"Why," said Kitty, impressed with the greatness of her own idea, "let's have a picnic!"

"Picnic!" cried Marjorie, "before breakfast! At half-past five in the morning! Kit, you're crazy!"

"No, I'm not crazy," said Kitty, seriously, and Molly broke in, "Of course she isn't! It's a grand idea!"

"But you can't have a picnic without things to eat," objected Marjorie.

"We'll have things to eat," declared Kitty, calmly.

"Where'll you get 'em?"

"Kitchen."

"Kit, you're a genius! Prob'ly Eliza's pantry is just chock-a-block with good things! And as I know they were made for us, we may as well eat some now."

Then Molly had an inspiration. "I'll tell you what," she cried, "let's go on the river! in the boat!"

CHAPTER VIII
AN EXCITING PICNIC

Molly's suggestion was so dazzling that Midget and Kitty were struck dumb for a moment. Then Marjorie said, "No, Grandma won't let us girls go on the river alone, and Carter isn't up yet."

"Let's throw pebbles and wake him up," said Molly.

"No," said Kitty, "it's too bad to wake him up early, because he needs his rest. He has to work hard all day, and he has the rheumatism besides. But I'll tell you what," and again Kitty's face glowed with a great idea; "let's go and throw pebbles at King's window, and make him take us out rowing."

"Kitty, getting up early in the morning agrees with your brain!" declared Marjorie. "We'll do just that,—and while King is dressing, we'll pack a basket of things to eat. Oh, gorgeous! Come on, girls!"

And clasping hands, the three ran away toward Grandma Sherwood's house.

"What about Stella?" asked Marjorie, as they passed her house.

"Oh, don't try to get her," said Molly; "she'd be scared to death if you pebbled her, and her mother and father would think the house was on fire or something."

So Stella was not included in the picnic, and the three conspirators ran on, and never paused until they were beneath King's window.

"You don't need a whole handful for him," advised Kitty. "I expect he's awake, anyway, and one pebble will make him come to the window. See, the window's open anyway; we can just fling a pebble in."

"If we can aim straight enough," said Molly.

After one or two vain attempts, Kitty sent a good-sized pebble straight through the open window, and it landed on the floor straight beside King's bed.

In another moment a tousled head and a pair of shoulders, humped into a bathrobe, appeared at the window.

Seeing the girls, King's face broke into a broad grin. "Well, you do beat all!" he cried. "Have you been out all night?"

"No," called Kitty, "we're just playing around in the morning. It's perfectly lovely out, King, and we're going to have a picnic, rowing on the river. But we can't go unless you'll come too, so bob into your clothes and come, won't you?"

"You bet I will! Isn't anybody up?"

"Nobody but us," said Marjorie; "so don't make any noise. Slide down the back stairs and through the kitchen."

"Got any feed for your picnic?"

"We're going to get some. You hurry down and we'll be ready."

"All right," and the tousled head disappeared. The girls went noiselessly into the kitchen and on through into the pantry. As Marjorie had surmised, the pantry shelves were well-stocked, and they found doughnuts, little pies, and cold chicken in abundance. Kitty found a goodly-sized basket, and remembering King's appetite, they packed it well.

"Here's some hard-boiled eggs," cried Marjorie, "let's take these."

"I 'spect Eliza wants them for salad or something," said Kitty, "but she can boil more. We must take some milk, Midget."

"Yes, here's a big pitcher full. Let's put it in a tin pail to carry it.
The milkman will be here in time for breakfast."
And so when King came softly downstairs, with his shoes in his hand, he found the luncheon basket packed, and the feminine portion of the picnic all ready to start.

"Good work!" he said, approvingly, as he lifted the basket, greatly pleased with its size and weight.

Molly carried the milk pail, Kitty some glasses and Marjorie some napkins and forks, for she was of a housewifely nature, and liked dainty appointments.

"Maybe we ought to leave a note or something," said Kitty, as they started.

"Saying we've eloped," said King, grinning.

"Don't let's bother," said Marjorie; "they'll know we're just out playing somewhere, and we'll be back by breakfast time,—it isn't six o'clock yet."

"You won't want any breakfast after all this stuff," said Molly, whose appetite was not as robust as the Maynards'.

"'Deed we will!" declared King; "this little snack is all right for six o'clock, but I have an engagement at eight in the dining-room."

They trudged along to the boathouse, and, as they might have expected, found it locked.

"I'll get it," said Molly; "I'm the swiftest runner, and I know where the key hangs in Carter's workshop."

King watched Molly admiringly as she flew across the grass, her long, thin, black legs flinging out behind her with incredible quickness.

"Jingo, she can run!" he exclaimed, and indeed it seemed but a moment before Molly flashed back again with the key.

The quartet was soon in the boat, and with a few strokes, King pulled out into mid-stream.

"Let's have the picnic first," he said, shipping his oars. "I can't row when I'm so hungry. This morning air gives a fellow an appetite."

"It does so," agreed Marjorie; "and we girls have been out 'most an hour.
I'm 'bout starved."
So they held a very merry picnic breakfast, while the boat drifted along with the current, and the cold chicken and biscuits rapidly disappeared.

"Now, where do you girls want to go?" asked King, as, the last crumb finished, Kitty carefully packed the napkins and glasses back in the basket.

"Oh, let's go to Blossom Banks," said Marjorie, "that is, if there's time enough."

"We'll go down that way, anyhow," said King, "and if it gets late we'll come back before we get there. Anybody got a watch?"

Nobody had, but all agreed they wouldn't stay out very long, so on they went, propelled by King's long, strong strokes down toward Blossom Banks.

It was a delightful sensation, because it was such a novel one. To row on the river at six o'clock in the morning was a very different proposition from rowing later in the day. Molly and Marjorie sat together in the stern, and Kitty lay curled up in the bow, with her hands behind her head, dreamily gazing into the morning sky.

"Do you remember, Molly," said Midget, "how we went out with Carter one day, and he scolded us so because we bobbed about and paddled our hands in the water?"

"Yes, I remember," and Molly laughed at the recollection. "Let's dabble our hands now. May we, King?"

"Sure! I guess I can keep this boat right side up if you girls do trail your hands in the water."

And so the two merry maidens dabbled their hands in the water, and growing frolicsome, shook a spray over each other, and even flirted drops into King's face. The boy laughed good-naturedly, and retaliated by splashing a few drops on them with the tip end of his oar.

King was fond of rowing, and was clever at it, and being a large, strong boy, it tired him not at all. Moreover, the boat was a light, round-bottomed affair that rowed easily, and was not at all hard to manage.

King's foolery roused the spirit of mischief in the two girls, and faster and faster flew the drops of water from one to another of the merrymakers.

"No fair splashing!" cried King. "Just a spray of drops goes."

"All right," agreed Marjorie, who was also a stickler for fair play, and though she dashed the water rapidly, she sent merely a flying spray, and not a drenching handful. But Molly was not so punctilious. She hadn't the same instinct of fairness that the Maynards had, and half intentionally, half by accident, she flung a handful of water straight in King's face.

This almost blinded the boy, and for a moment he lost control of his oar. An involuntary move on his part, due to the shock of the water in his face, sent the blade of one oar down deep, and as he tried to retrieve it, it splashed a whole wave all over Molly.

But Molly thought King intended to do this, and that it was merely part of the game, so with one of her lightning-like movements, she grasped the blade of the oar in retaliation. The oar being farther away than she thought, and rapidly receding, caused her to lean far over the boat, and in his effort to get his oar again in position, King, too, leaned over the side.

The result was exactly what might have been expected. The narrow, clinker-built boat capsized, and in a moment the four children were struggling in the water.

Even as the boat went over, King realized what had happened, and realized, too, that he was responsible for the safety of the three girls. With fine presence of mind he threw his arm over the keel of the upturned boat and shouted, "It's all right, girls! Just hang on to the boat this way, and you won't go down."

Marjorie and Molly understood at once, and did exactly as King told them. They were terribly frightened, and were almost strangled, but they realized the emergency, and struggled to get their arms up over the boat in the manner King showed them.

But Kitty did not so quickly respond to orders. She had not been paying any attention to the merry war going on in the stern of the boat, and when she was suddenly thrown out into the water, she could not at first collect her scattered senses. King's words seemed to convey no meaning to her, and to his horror, the boy saw his sister sink down under the water.

"Hang on like fury, you two girls!" he shouted to Marjorie and Molly, and then he made a dive for Kitty.

King was a good swimmer, but, hampered by his clothing, and frightened terribly by Kitty's disappearance, he could not do himself justice. But he caught hold of Kitty's dress, and by good fortune both rose to the surface. King grabbed for the boat, but it slipped away from him, and the pair went down again.

At this Marjorie screamed. She had been trying to be brave, yet the sight of her brother and sister being, as she feared, drowned, was too much for her.

"Hush up, Marjorie!" cried Molly. "You just keep still and hang on! I can swim!"

With an eel-like agility Molly let go of the boat, and darted through the water. She was really a good swimmer, and her thin, muscular little limbs struck out frantically in all directions. Diving swiftly, she bumped against Kitty, and grasping her arm firmly, she began to tread water rapidly. As King was doing this on the other side of Kitty, the three shot up to the surface, and King and Molly grasped the boat with firm hands, holding Kitty between them.

Kitty was limp, but conscious; and though King was exhausted, he held on to Kitty, and held on to the boat, with a desperate grip.

"Wait a minute, girls," he gasped, sputtering and stammering; "I'll be all right in a minute. Now as long as you hold fast to the boat, you know you can't drown! How are you getting along, Mops?"

"All right," called Marjorie from the other side of the boat; "but I want to come over there by you."

"Don't you do it! You stay there and balance the boat. It's lucky you're a heavyweight! Now you girls do exactly as I tell you to."

King did not mean to be dictatorial, but he was getting his breath back, and he knew that although their heads were above water, still strenuous measures were necessary.

"What shall we do?" shouted Marjorie.

"Well, we must try to get this boat to shore. And as we're much nearer the other shore than our own side, we'll try to get it over there, for we don't want to cross the river. Now hang on tight, and wiggle your feet like paddles. If you kick out hard enough, I think we can get the old thing ashore."

It wasn't an easy task, nor a quick one, but after a while, by vigorous kicking, in accordance with King's continued directions, they did succeed in reaching shallow water.

"Now we can walk," said King, "but we may as well hang on to the boat and not let her drift away."

So half scrambling, half crawling, the children pushed through the shallow water and up on to the shore, dragging the upturned boat with them. The shore just here was shelving and sandy, otherwise it is doubtful if they could have reached it at all. But at last four shivering, dripping children stood on solid ground, and looked at each other.

"You're an old trump, King," cried Marjorie, flinging her arms around her brother's neck, and kissing his wet cheeks; "you're a hero, and a life-saver, and a Victoria Cross, and everything!"

"There, there, Midget, come off! I didn't do anything much; Molly here did the most, but, thank goodness, we all got out alive! Now what shall we do next?"

Kitty had recovered entirely from her dazed and stunned feeling, and was again her practical and helpful self.

"We must run," she said, "we must run like sixty! That's the only way to keep from catching cold in these wet clothes!"

"Can't we build a fire, and dry ourselves?" asked Molly, who was shivering with cold.

"No, of course not," said Kitty, "for we haven't any matches, and if we had they'd be soaked. No, we must run as hard as we can tear along this bank until we get opposite Grandma's house, and then they'll have to come over and get us somehow."

"How'll they know we're there?" asked Molly.

"I'll yell," said Marjorie, quite confident of her powers in this direction. "I'll yell,—and I just know I can make Carter hear me!"

"I'll bet you can!" said King. "Come on then, let's run. Take hold of hands."

With King and Midget at either end of the line, and the other two between, they ran!

CHAPTER IX
ANCIENT FINERY
When the children reached the big open field that was just across the river from Grandma Sherwood's, although their clothes had ceased dripping, they were far from dry, and they all shivered in the keen morning air.

"Yell away, Mopsy," cried King. "You can make Carter hear if anybody can."

So Marjorie yelled her very best ear-splitting shrieks.

"Car-ter! Car-ter!" she screamed, and the others gazed at her in admiration.

"Well, you can yell!" said Molly. "I expect my people will hear that!"

After two or three more screams, they saw Carter come running down toward the boathouse. Looking across the river, he saw the four children frantically waving their hands and beckoning to him.

"For the land's sake! What is going on now?" he muttered, hurrying down to the bank as fast as his rheumatic old legs would carry him.

"And the boat's gone!" he exclaimed; "now, however did them children get over there without no boat? By the looks of their wet clothes they must have swum over, but I don't believe they could do that. Hey, there!" he shouted, making a megaphone of his hands.

"Come over and get us," Marjorie yelled back, and beginning to realize the situation, Carter went into the boathouse and began to take out the other boat. This was an old flat-bottomed affair, which had been unused since Uncle Steve bought the new boat.

"Most prob'ly she leaks like a sieve," he muttered, as he untied the boat and pushed it out; "but I've nothing else to bring the young rascals home in. So they'll have to bail while I row."

Carter was soon in the old boat, and pulling it across the river. As he had expected, it leaked badly, but he was sure he could get the children home in it.

"Come on now!" he cried, as he beached the boat, and jumped out. "For the land's sake, how did you get so wet? But don't stop to tell me now! Just pile in the boat, and let me get you home to a fire and some dry clothes. You'll all have to bail, for she leaks something awful."

Not waiting for a second invitation, the damp quartet scrambled into the boat, and Carter pulled off. The old man had provided tin cans, and the children bailed all the way over, for it was necessary to do so to keep the boat afloat.

As they went, Marjorie told Carter the whole story, "and you see," she concluded, "we didn't do anything wrong, for we're always allowed to go in a boat if King is with us."

"Oh, no, Miss Mischief, you didn't do anything wrong! Of course it wasn't wrong to jump about in the boat and carry on until you upset it! It's a marvel you weren't all drowned."

"It is so!" said King, who realized more fully than the others the danger they had been in. "Why, there's Uncle Steve on the dock, and Father, too; I wonder if they heard Midget scream."

"If they were within a mile and not stone deaf they couldn't help hearing her," declared Carter. He rowed as fast as he could, and he made the children keep hard at work bailing, not only to get the water out of the boat, but because he feared if they sat still they'd take cold.

At last they reached the dock, and Uncle Steve and Mr. Maynard assisted them out of the boat.

It was no time then for questions or comments, and Uncle Steve simply issued commands.

"Molly," he said, "you scamper home as fast as you can fly! We have enough to attend to with our own brood. Scoot, now, and don't stop until you reach your own kitchen fire, and tell your mother what has happened. As for you Maynards, you fly to Grandma's kitchen, and see what Eliza can do for you."

Molly flew off across the lawns to her own house, running so swiftly that she was out of sight in a moment. Then the Maynards, obeying Uncle Steve's command, ran to the kitchen door, and burst in upon Eliza as she was just finishing the breakfast preparations.

"Howly saints!" she cried. "If it wasn't that I always ixpict yees to come in drownded, I'd be sheared to death! But if yees weren't in this mess, ye'd be in some other. Such childher I niver saw!"

Eliza's tirade probably would have been longer, but just then Grandma and Mrs. Maynard came into the kitchen.
"Been for a swim?" asked Mrs. Maynard, pleasantly.

"Almost been drowned," said Kitty, rushing into her mother's arm, greatly to the detriment of her pretty, fresh morning dress.

As soon as Mrs. Maynard realized that her brood had really been in danger, she gathered all three forlorn, wet little figures into her arms at once, thankful that they were restored to her alive.

Then breakfast was delayed while Grandma and Mother Maynard provided dry clothing, and helped the children to transform themselves once more into respectable citizens.

"Now tell us all about it, but one at a time," said Uncle Steve, as at last breakfast was served, and they all sat round the table. "King, your version first."

"Well, we all went out for an early morning row, and somehow we got to carrying on, and that round-bottomed boat tipped so easily, that somehow we upset it."

"It's a wonder you weren't drowned!" exclaimed Grandma.

"I just guess it is!" agreed Marjorie; "and we would have been, only King saved us! Kitty was 'most drowned, and King went down in the water and fished her up, and Molly helped a good deal, and I stayed on the other side and balanced the boat."

"The girls were all plucky," declared King, "and the whole thing was an accident. It wasn't wrong for us to go out rowing early in the morning, was it, Father?"

"I don't think it was the hour of the day that made the trouble, my son. But are you sure you did nothing else that was wrong?"

"I did," confessed Marjorie, frankly. "I splashed water, and then the others splashed water, and that's how we came to upset."

"Yes, that was the trouble," said Mr. Maynard; "you children are quite old enough to know that you must sit still in a boat. Especially a round-bottomed boat, and a narrow one at that."

"It was Molly's fault more than Midget's," put in Kitty, who didn't want her adored sister to be blamed more than she deserved.

"Well, never mind that," said Marjorie, generously ignoring Molly's part in the disaster. "There's one thing sure, Kitty wasn't a bit to blame."

"No," said King, "Kit sat quiet as a mouse. She wouldn't upset an airship. Mopsy and I were the bad ones, as usual, and I think we ought to be punished."

"I think so, too," said Mr. Maynard, "but as this is a vacation holiday I hate to spoil it with punishments, so I'm going to wait until you cut up your next naughty trick, and then punish you for both at once. Is that a good plan, Mother?"

"Yes," said Mrs. Maynard, looking fondly at the culprits, "but I want to stipulate that the children shall not go out in the boat again without some grown person with them."

"I'm glad of that," said Marjorie, "for no matter how hard I try I don't believe I could sit perfectly still in a boat, so I'll be glad to have some grownup go along."

"That's my chance," exclaimed Uncle Steve, "I'll take you any time you want to go, Midget, and I'll guarantee to bring you back without a ducking."

"Thank you, Uncle Steve," said Marjorie; "shall we go right after breakfast?"

"Not quite so soon as that, but perhaps to-morrow. By the way, kiddies, what do you think of having a little party while you're here? That would keep you out of mischief for half a day."

"Oh, lovely!" exclaimed Marjorie. "Uncle Steve, you do have the beautifullest ideas! What kind of a party?"

"Any kind that isn't a ducking party."

"But we don't know anybody much to invite," said Kitty.

"Yes, I know quite a few," said Marjorie, "and King knows several boys; and anyway, Molly and Stella will help us make out a list. How many shall we have, Uncle Steve?"

"About twenty, I think, and I'll have a hand at that list myself. I know most of the children around here. This afternoon get Molly and Stella to come in after school, and we'll make the list. We can send the invitations to-night, and have the party day after to-morrow. That's warning enough for such young, young people."

"It seems to be your party, Steve," said Mrs. Maynard, smiling; "can't I help you with the arrangements?"

"Yes, indeed; you and Mother can look after the feast part of it, but the rest I'll attend to myself."

After breakfast the children were advised to stay indoors for a while, lest they get into more mischief, and also until their elders felt that there was no danger of their taking cold.

"Lucky we didn't have Rosy Posy with us," said King, picking up his smallest sister, and tossing her up in the air.

"Don't speak of it," said his mother, turning pale at the thought; "and don't ever take the baby on your escapades. She's too little to go through the dangers that you older ones persist in getting into."

"Oh, we don't persist," said Marjorie, "the dangers just seem to come to us without our looking for them."

"They do seem to, Midget," agreed Uncle Steve. "But you all seem to have a happy-go-lucky way of getting out of them, and I think you're a pretty good bunch of children after all."

"Listen to that!" exclaimed King, proudly, strutting about the room, elated with the compliment. "It's worth while having an uncle who says things like that to you," and the others willingly agreed with him.

Kept in the house, the children wandered about in search of amusement. Kitty curled herself up on a sofa, with a book, saying she was determined to keep out of mischief for once.

"Let's go up in the attic," said Midget to King, "and hunt over our old toys that are put away up there. We might find some nice game."

"All right, come on," and in a minute the two were scrambling up the attic stairs.

"Gracious! look at that big chest. I never saw that before. Wonder what's in it," said Marjorie, pausing before a big cedar chest.

"Is it locked?" said King, and lifting the lid he discovered it wasn't.

But it was filled to the brim with old-fashioned garments of queer old
Quaker cut.
"Wouldn't it be fun to dress up in these," cried King.

"Yes," assented Marjorie, "but I'm not going to do it, until we ask Grandma. I've had enough mischief for one day."
So King ran downstairs and asked Grandma, and soon came running back.

"She says we may," he announced briefly, "so let's choose our rigs."

They lifted out the quaint, old-fashioned clothes, and found there were both men's and women's garments among them.

"Where do you suppose they came from?" asked Marjorie.

"Grandma said some old relative in Philadelphia sent her the chest, some time ago, but she's never opened it."

They tried on various costumes, and pranced around the attic, pretending they were ladies and gentlemen of bygone days.

Finally King tried on a woman's dress. It just fitted him, and when he added a silk Shaker bonnet and a little shoulder shawl, the effect was so funny that Marjorie screamed with laughter.

"All you want," she said, "is some false hair in the front of that bonnet, and you'll be a perfect little old lady."

Then Marjorie ran down to Grandma, and asked her for some of her false puffs, and getting them, flew back to the attic again, and deftly pinned them inside of King's bonnet, transforming him into a sweet-faced Quaker lady.

Then Marjorie arrayed herself as another Quaker lady, drawing her hair down in smooth bands over her ears, which greatly changed the expression of her face, and made her look much older. Each carried an old-fashioned silk reticule, and together they went downstairs. After parading before their admiring relatives, they decided to play a joke on Eliza. She had not yet seen them, so they slipped downstairs and out the front door, and then closing it softly behind them, they rang the bell.

Eliza came to the door, and utterly failed to recognize the children.

"Does Mrs. Sherwood live here?" asked King, in a thin, disguised voice.

"Yes, ma'am," said Eliza, not knowing the children, "but—" gazing in surprise at the quaint, old-fashioned dresses and bobbing bonnets.

"Please tell her her two aunts from Philadelphia are here," said Marjorie, but she could not disguise her voice as well as King, and Eliza suddenly recognized it.

"Two aunts from Phillydelphy, is it?" she said. "More likes it's too loonytics from Crazyland! What will ye mischiefs be cuttin' up next! But, faith, ye're the bonny ould ladies, and if ye'll come in and take a seat, I'll tell the missus ye're here."

But, having fooled Eliza, the fun was over in that direction, and the Quaker ladies trotted away to make a call on Carter.

Just at first he didn't know them, and thought the two ladies were coming to see him. But in a moment he saw who they were, and the good-natured man entered at once into the game.

CHAPTER X
CALLING AT THE SCHOOLHOUSE

"Good-morning, ladies," he said, bowing gravely, "I'm very pleased to see you. May I ask your names?"

"Mrs. William Penn and Mrs. Benjamin Franklin," said Marjorie, "and we have come to look at your flowers."

"Yes, ma'am; they do be fine this year, ma'am. Happen you raise flowers yourself?"

"No, not much," said King, "we don't raise anything."

"Except when you raise the mischief," declared Carter, laughing at the prim faces before him. "I'm thinkin' if you'd always wear those sober-colored dresses you mightn't lead such a rambunctious life."

"That's so," said King, kicking at his skirts. "But they're not easy to get around in."

"I think they are," said Marjorie, gracefully swishing the long folds of her silk skirt. "Come on, King, let's go over and see Stella; we haven't seen her yet."

"Miss Stella's gone to school," Carter informed them. "I saw her go by with her books just before nine o'clock. And if you ladies can excuse me now, I'll be going back to my work. If so be ye fall in the river or anything, just you scream, Miss Marjorie, and I'll come and fish you out."

"We don't fall in twice in one day," said Marjorie, with dignity, and the two Quaker ladies trailed away across the lawn.

They went down into the orchard, to pay a visit to Breezy Inn. This was Marjorie's tree-house which Uncle Steve had had built for her the year before.

But the rope ladder was not there, so they could not go up, and they wandered on, half hoping they might meet somebody who would really think they were Quaker ladies. Crossing the orchard, they came out on one of the main streets of the town, and saw not far away, the school which Stella and Molly attended.

Marjorie had a sudden inspiration. "Let's go to the school," she said, "and ask for Stella and Molly!"

"Only one of them," amended King; "which one?"

"Stella, then. We'll go to the front door, and we'll probably see the janitor, and we'll ask him to call Stella Martin down."

"I think we'd better send for Molly."

"No, Molly would make such a racket. Stella's so much quieter, and I don't want to make any trouble."

They reached the schoolhouse, which was a large brick building of three or four stories. The front door was a rather impressive portal, and the children went up the steps and rang the bell.

"You do the talking, King," said Marjorie. "You can make your voice sound just like an old lady."

The janitor appeared in answer to their ring, and looked greatly amazed to see two old Quaker ladies on the doorstep. The children kept their heads down, and the large bonnets shaded their faces.

"We want to see Miss Stella Martin," said King, politely, and the clever boy made his voice sound like that of an elderly lady.

"Yes'm," said the janitor, a little bewildered. "Will you come in?"

"No," said King, "we won't come in, thank you. Please ask Miss Stella Martin to come down here. Her two aunts from Philadelphia want to see her."

The janitor partly closed the door, and went upstairs to Stella's classroom.

"We fooled him all right!" chuckled King, "but what do you suppose Stella will say?"

"I don't know," said Midget, thoughtfully; "you never can tell what Stella will do. She may think it's a great joke, and she may burst out crying. She's such a funny girl."

In a moment Stella came down. The janitor was with her, and opened the door for her. As she saw the two Quaker figures her face expressed only blank bewilderment.

"Who are you?" she asked, bluntly. "I haven't any aunts in Philadelphia."

"Oh, yes, you have," said King, in his falsetto voice, "Don't you remember your dear Aunt Effie and Aunt Lizzie?"

"No, I don't," declared Stella, and then as she showed signs of being frightened, and perhaps crying, Marjorie came to the rescue.

She hated to explain the joke before the janitor, but he looked good-natured, and after all it was only a joke. So she threw back her head, and smiled at Stella, saying, "Then do you remember your Aunt Marjorie Maynard?"

"Marjorie!" exclaimed Stella. "What are you doing in such funny clothes? And who is this with you,—Kitty?"

"No," said King, "it's Kingdon. I'm Marjorie's brother, and we're out on a little lark."

"How did you ever dare come here?" and Stella's startled gaze rested on them, and then on the janitor.

The janitor was a good-natured man, but he felt that this performance was not in keeping with school discipline, and he felt he ought to send the children away at once. But Marjorie smiled at him so winningly that he could not speak sternly to her.

"I guess you'd better run along now," he said; "the principal wouldn't like it if he saw you."

"Yes, we're going now," said Marjorie, "but I just wanted to speak to Stella a minute. We're going to have a party, Stella, and I want you to come over this afternoon and tell us who to invite."

"All right," said Stella; "I'll come right after school. And now do go away. If my teacher should see you she'd scold me."

"She'd have no right to," said King. "You couldn't help our coming."

"No, but I can help staying here and talking to you. Now I must go back to my classroom."

"Skip along, then," said Marjorie, and then turning to the janitor, she added, "and will you please ask Miss Molly Moss to come down."

"That I will not!" declared the man. "I've been pretty good to you two kids, and now you'd better make a getaway, or I'll have to report to the principal."

"Oh, we're going," said Marjorie, hastily; "and don't mention our call to the principal, because it might make trouble for Stella, though I don't see why it should."

"Well, I won't say anything about it," and the janitor smiled at them kindly as he closed the door.

The pair went home chuckling, and when they reached the house it was nearly lunch time. So they came to the table in their Quaker garb, and created much merriment by pretending to be guests of the family.

Stella and Molly both came after school, and the list for the party invitations was soon made out. Uncle Steve wrote the invitations, and sent them to the mail, but he would not divulge any of his plans for the party, and though Midget was impatient to know, she could get no idea of what the plays or games were to be.

But it was not long to wait for the day of the party itself. The guests were invited from three to six in the afternoon, and though the Maynards knew some of them, there were a number of strangers among the company. However, Stella and Molly knew them all, and it did not take long for the Maynards to feel acquainted with them.

The first game was very amusing. Uncle Steve presented each child with a Noah's Ark. These were of the toy variety usually seen, but they were all empty.

"You must find animals for yourselves," said Uncle Steve, who was never happier than when entertaining children. "They are hidden all about, in the drawing-room, library, dining-room, and hall. You may not go upstairs, or in the kitchen, but anywhere else in the house you may search for animals to fill your arks. Now scamper and see who can get the most."

The children scampered, and all agreed that hunting wild animals was a great game. It was lots more fun than a peanut hunt, and they found elephants, lions, and tigers tucked away behind window curtains and sofa pillows, under tables and chairs, and even behind the pictures on the walls.

There were so many animals that each one succeeded in filling his or her ark, and after they had declared they could find no more, each child was told to take the ark home as a souvenir of Marjorie's party.

"The next game," said Uncle Steve, as they all sat round, awaiting his directions, "is out of doors, so perhaps you had better put on your coats and hats."

"Oh, Uncle Steve," said Marjorie, "the air is so soft and warm, I'm sure we don't need wraps."

"Yes, you do," said Uncle Steve; "this is a peculiar game, and you must have your coats on."

So the children trooped upstairs, and soon returned garbed for outdoors, and two by two they followed Uncle Steve in a long procession. Mr. Maynard was with them, too, but Uncle Steve was general manager, and told everybody what to do.

He led them across the lawns, down through the orchard, and then they came to a large plot of soft, newly-dug earth. It was a sandy soil and not at all muddy, and the children wondered what kind of a game could take place in a ploughed field.

"It has just been discovered," Uncle Steve began, "that this field you see before you is the place where Captain Kidd buried his treasures! For many years the site was undiscovered, but documents have been found recently, proving beyond all doubt that the greater part of his vast treasure was concealed in this particular piece of ground. Of course, if this were generally known, all sorts of companies and syndicates would be formed to dig for it. But I have carefully kept it secret from the world at large, because I wanted you children to be the first ones to dig for it. Bring the spades, please, Carter, and let us set to work at once."

So Carter brought twenty small spades, and gave one to each child present.

"Now," said Uncle Steve, "dig wherever you like, all over the field, and when you find any buried treasure, dig it up, but if it is tied up in a parcel, do not open it. Every one finding any treasure must bring it, and put it in this wheelbarrow, and then, if you choose, you may go back and dig for more."

This was indeed a novel game, and girls and boys alike began to dig with enthusiasm.

Marjorie worked like mad. The dirt flew right and left, and she dug so hard and fast that she almost blistered her palms.

"Slow and sure is a better rule, Midget," said her uncle, who was watching her. "Look at Kitty, she has dug quite as much as you without making any fuss about it."

"Oh, I have to work fast, Uncle Steve, 'cause I'm having such a good time! If I didn't fling this spade around hard, I couldn't express my enjoyment; and oh, Uncle, I've struck a treasure!"

Sure enough, Marjorie's spade had come in contact with what seemed to be a tin box. It was quite a large box and was strongly tied with lots of cord, and on it was pasted a paper with the legend, "This treasure was buried by Captain Kidd. It is of great value."

"It is a treasure, it is!" cried Marjorie, and eagerly she wielded her spade to get the box free. At last she succeeded, and picking it up from the dirt, carried it to the wheelbarrow.

Two or three other children also brought treasures they had found, and this encouraged the others so that they dug deeper.

Shouts of glee rang out from one or another as more and more boxes of treasure were unearthed, and the pile of boxes in the wheelbarrow grew higher every moment. The boxes were of all shapes and sizes. They were all carefully tied up with lots of string and paper, and they all bore testimony in large printed letters that they had been buried by Captain Kidd and his band of pirates. King unearthed a large box two or three feet square, but very flat and shallow. He could not imagine what it might contain, but he piled it on the wheelbarrow with the others.

After twenty pieces of treasure had been dug up, Uncle Steve declared that they had emptied the field, and he led the children back to the house. Carter followed with the wheelbarrow, and they all gathered in the little enclosed porch that had been furnished especially for Marjorie the summer before. With a whiskbroom, Carter brushed off any dirt still clinging to the treasures, and piled them up on a table.

Then calling the children by name. Uncle Steve invited each one to select a box of treasure for his or her very own. As it was impossible to judge by the shape of the box what it contained, great merriment was caused by the surprises which ensued.

The treasures were all dainty and pretty gifts; there were books, games, toys, fancy boxes, and pretty souvenirs of many sorts. If a boy received a gift appropriate for a girl, or vice versa, they made a happy exchange, and everybody was more than satisfied.

After this, they were summoned to the dining-room for the feast, and a merry feast it was. Eliza had used her best skill in the making of dainty sandwiches and little cakes with pink and white icing. Then there were jellies and fruits, and, best of all, in Kitty's eyes, most delightful ice cream. It was in individual shapes, and each child had a duck, or a chicken, or a flower, or a fruit beautifully modelled and daintily colored.

The guests went away with a box of treasure under one arm and a Noah's ark under the other, and they all declared, as they said good-bye, that it was the nicest party they had ever seen, and they wished the Maynard children lived at their Grandmother's all the year around.

CHAPTER XI
A CHANCE ACQUAINTANCE
All of the Maynards were sorry when the time came to leave Grandma Sherwood's. But they had still three weeks of their trip before them, and many places yet to be visited. Kitty was almost tempted to stay, since she was coming back in June anyway, and she wasn't quite so fond of travelling about as King and Midget were. But they would not hear of this, and persuaded Kitty to go on the trip, and return to Grandma Sherwood's later.

So on a fair, sunshiny May morning, the big car started once more on its travels, with half a dozen Maynards packed in it. They were waving good-byes, and calling back messages of farewell, and the car rolled away, leaving Grandma and Uncle Steve watching them out of sight.

Their next destination was New York City, where they were to make a short visit at Grandma Maynard's.

"Isn't it funny," Marjorie said, voicing the sentiment of many older travellers, "that when you leave one place you sort of forget it,—and your thoughts fly ahead to the next place you're going."

"It's so long since I've been at Grandma Maynard's," said Kitty, "and I was so little when I was there, that I hardly remember it at all."

"It isn't half as much fun as Grandma Sherwood's," declared King, and then Marjorie, afraid lest her father should feel hurt, added quickly, "But it's very nice indeed, and Grandma and Grandpa Maynard are lovely. The only reason we have more fun at Grandma Sherwood's is because we don't have to be quite so careful of our manners and customs."

"Well, it won't hurt you, Midget," said her mother, "to have a little experience in that line; and I do hope, children, you will behave yourselves, and not go to cutting up any of your mischief or jinks."

"Kit will be our star exhibit," said King, "she'll have to do the manners for the family."

"I'll do my share," said Kitty, taking him literally, "but unless you two behave, I can't do it all. If you go to pulling hair-ribbons and neckties off each other, Grandma Maynard will think you're Hottentots!"

"I will be good, dear Mother," said King, with such an angelic expression on his face that Mrs. Maynard felt sure he was in a specially roguish mood; and though she thought her children were the dearest in the world, yet she knew they had a propensity for getting into mischief just when she wanted them to act most decorously.

But she said no more, for very often special admonitions resulted in special misbehavior.

They were spinning along a lovely country road, which ran across that portion of New Jersey, and the children found much to interest them in the scenes they passed. Mr. Maynard liked to travel rather slowly, and as it neared noon they stopped at a hotel for luncheon. Here they stayed for some time, and the children were delighted to find that there were several other children living at the hotel, and they soon became acquainted.

One girl, about Marjorie's age, named Ethel Sinclair, seemed an especially nice child, and Mrs. Maynard was glad to have Marjorie play with her.

She was sitting on the veranda embroidering, and this interested Marjorie, for all the girls she knew of her own age liked to run and play better than to sit and sew.

But when Ethel showed them her work, Kitty and Marjorie, and even King, took an interest in looking at it. It was a large piece of white linen, about a yard square, neatly hemstitched, and all over it were names of people.

Ethel explained that she asked any one whom she chose to write an autograph on the cloth in pencil, and then afterward she worked them very carefully with red cotton, taking very small stitches that the names might be clear and legible.

"But what's it for?" asked King, with a boy's ignorance of such matters.

"It's a teacloth," said Ethel, "to cover a tea table, you know."

"But you don't have afternoon tea, do you?" asked Marjorie, for Ethel, like herself, was only twelve.

"No, but I'm going to use it for a tablecover in my bedroom, and perhaps when I grow older I can use it for a teacloth."

Ethel was a prim-mannered child, and had apparently been brought up in a conventional manner, but Marjorie liked her, and stayed talking with her, while King and Kitty went off to explore the gardens.

"I wish I could make one," went on Marjorie to Ethel, "where did you get the linen?"

"There's a little shop just down the road, and they have the squares already hemstitched. It would be nice for you to make one, for you could get so many names as you go on your trip."

"So I could; I'm going to ask mother if I may buy one. Will you go with me, Ethel?"

Ethel went gladly, and when the girls showed the teacloth to Mrs. Maynard, she approved of the whole plan, for she wanted Marjorie to become more fond of her needle, and this work would be an incentive to do so.

So she gave Marjorie the money for the purchase, and the two girls trotted away to the little shop which was not far from the hotel.

Marjorie found a square just like Ethel's, and bought it with a decidedly grownup feeling.

"I don't like to sew much," she confessed to Ethel, as they walked back.
"I've tried it a little, but I'd rather read or play."
"But this isn't like regular sewing, and it's such fun to see the names grow right under your eyes. They're so much prettier after they're worked in red than when they're just written in pencil."

"Wouldn't they be prettier still worked in white?" asked Marjorie.

"No; I saw one that way once, and the names don't show at all,—you can hardly read them. Red is the best, and it doesn't fade when it's washed."

Marjorie had bought red cotton at the shop, and she showed her purchases to her mother with great delight.

"They're fine," said Mrs. Maynard, approvingly. "Now why don't you ask Ethel to write her name, and then you can always remember that hers was the first one on the cloth."

"Oh, that will be lovely!" cried Marjorie. "Will you, Ethel?"

"Yes, indeed," and getting a pencil, Ethel wrote her name in a large, plain, childish hand.

"You must always ask people to write rather large," she advised, "because it's awfully hard to work the letters if they're too small."

Then Ethel lent Marjorie her needle and thimble so that she might do a few stitches by way of practice.

But it was not so easy for Marjorie as for Ethel, and her stitches did not look nearly so nice and neat. However, Mrs. Maynard said that she felt sure Marjorie's work would improve after she had done more of it, and she thanked Ethel for her assistance in the matter.

Then Ethel's mother appeared, and the two ladies were made acquainted, and then it was luncheon time, and the Maynards all went to the dining-room.

"I think the most fun of the whole trip is eating in restaurants," said Kitty. "I just love to look around, and see different tables and different people at them."

"It is fun," agreed King; "but I wouldn't want to live in a hotel all the time. I think it's more fun to be at home."

"So do I," said Marjorie. "Somehow, in a hotel, you feel sort of stiff and queer, and you never do at home."

"You needn't feel stiff and queer, Marjorie," said her father; "but of course there is a certain conventional restraint about a public dining-room that isn't necessary at home. I want you children to become accustomed to restaurants, and learn how to act polite and reserved, without being what Marjorie calls stiff and queer."

"Don't we act right, Father?" inquired Kitty, anxiously.

"Yes, you do very nicely, indeed. Your table manners are all right, and the less you think about the subject the better. This trip will give you a certain amount of experience, and anyway you have all your life to learn in. But I will ask you, children, to be on your good behavior at Grandma Maynard's. She is more difficult to please than Grandma Sherwood, but I want her to think my children are the best and the best-behaved in the whole world."

"How long shall we stay there, Father?" asked Marjorie.

"About three days. I'm sure you can exist that long without falling in the water or cutting up any pranks in the house."

"Is there any water to fall in?" asked King.

"No, there isn't. I used that as a figure of speech. But I'm sure if you try to be quiet and well-behaved children you can easily succeed."

"I'm sure we can," said Marjorie, heartily, and deep in her heart she registered a vow that she would succeed this time.

After luncheon was over, Pompton brought the car around, and they started off again. Marjorie bade Ethel good-bye with a feeling of regret that she did not live nearer, so she might have her for a friend. But she had her autograph as a souvenir, and she intended to work her tablecloth very neatly, so it would look as good as Ethel's.

The afternoon ride was not a long one, and before four o'clock they came in sight of the tall towers of the New York buildings.

The children had never approached the city in a motor car before, and were enthusiastic over the view of it. Mr. Maynard pointed out the different business buildings, some of which they already recognized. They had to cross a downtown ferry, and soon they were speeding north through the streets of crowded traffic.

As they neared Grandma Maynard's house in Fifth Avenue, Mrs. Maynard looked over her brood carefully to see if they were in proper order for presentation.

Except for slight evidences of travel, they all looked neat and tidy, and the girls' pretty motor garb was becoming and correct. Rosy Posy as usual, looked the pink of perfection, for the child had a knack of keeping herself dainty and fresh even in difficult circumstances.

Satisfied with her inspection, Mrs. Maynard gave them final injunctions to behave correctly, and then they reached the house.

The children had been there before, but they did not go often, and for the last two years the elder Maynards had been travelling abroad. So they felt almost like strangers as they entered the lofty and dimly lighted hall, to which they were admitted by an imposing-looking footman in livery.

Ushered into the reception room, the visitors found themselves in the presence of their host and hostess.

Grandma and Grandpa Maynard were most worthy and estimable people; but they were not very young, and they had lived all their lives in an atmosphere of convention and formality. They did not realize that this was different from the mode of living preferred by their son's family, and indeed they were so accustomed to their own ways that it never occurred to them that there were any others.

Mr. and Mrs. Maynard appreciated and understood all this, and accepted the situation as it stood.

But the children, impressed by the admonitions of their parents, and oppressed by the severe and rigid effects of the house, turned into quiet little puppets, quite different from their usual merry selves.

Although the elder Maynards' greetings were formal, Mr. and Mrs. Maynard, Jr., were cordial in their manner. Mr. Maynard shook his father heartily by the hand, and kissed his mother tenderly, and Mrs. Maynard did the same.

Marjorie endeavored to do exactly as her parents did, but as she began to chatter to her grandfather, Grandma Maynard told her that children should be seen and not heard, and bade her sit down on a sofa. The old lady had no intention of hurting Marjorie's feelings, but she meant exactly what she said, and it irritated her to hear a child chatter.

"And now," said Grandma Maynard, after the greetings were all over, "you would like to go to your rooms, I'm sure, and make ready for tea."

Decorously the children filed upstairs and were put in charge of maids who assisted them with their toilets.

Marjorie and Kitty were in the same room, but owing to the maids' presence, they could make no comments.

As the trunks had been sent ahead, they had fresh frocks in plenty, and soon, attired in stiff white kilted piqué, they went downstairs again.

Grandma Maynard nodded approval, and told them to sit down on the divan.

"Of course, you little girls don't drink tea," she said, as she seated herself behind the elaborately appointed tea-tray which the butler had brought in. "So I have milk for you."

This was entirely satisfactory, and as there were plenty of lovely little cakes and dainty sandwiches, the children felt there was no fault to be found with Grandma's hospitality, even though they were not allowed to talk.

King adapted himself rather more easily than the girls to this order of things, and he sat quietly in his chair, speaking only when he was spoken to; and though Marjorie knew he was fairly aching to shout and race around, yet he looked so demure that he almost made her laugh.

Not that she did! No, indeed, she knew better than that; but though she tried very hard to appear at her ease, her nature was so sensitive to mental atmosphere, that her cakes almost choked her.

Rosy Posy was perfectly at ease. The midget sat quietly, and accepted with benign grace the milk and crackers fed to her by one of the maids.

But at last the tea hour was over and the Maynards discovered that virtue is sometimes rewarded.

"You are most pleasant and amiable children," said Grandma Maynard, looking judicially at the quartet, "and you certainly have very good manners. I'm glad to see, Ed, that you have brought them up to be quiet and sedate. I detest noisy children."

"Yes, you are sensible, and not annoying to have around," agreed Grandpa Maynard, and the three older children smiled respectfully at the compliment, but offered no reply.

"And now," went on Grandpa Maynard, "I think that you should be amused for an hour. They don't sit up to dinner, of course, my dear?" he added, turning to his wife.

"Yes, we do!" was on the tip of Marjorie's tongue, but she checked the speech just in time, and said nothing.

"No, of course not," replied Grandma Maynard; "our dinner hour is eight, and that is too late for children. Besides, I have invited some guests to meet Ed and Helen. So the children will have supper in the small breakfast-room at half-past six, and meantime, as you say, we must give them some amusement."

King greatly wondered what these grandparents' idea of amusement would be, but Marjorie and Kitty had so little hope that it would be anything very enjoyable that they took little interest in it.

However, when it proved that the amusement was to be a ride in the park, it sounded rather attractive.

CHAPTER XII
AT GRANDMA MAYNARD'S

The ride in the park, though conducted under rather formal conditions, proved very enjoyable to the four young Maynards.

Grandpa Maynard's equipage was a Victoria with a span of fine horses. On the high front seat sat the coachman and footman in livery, who looked sufficiently dignified and responsible to take care of a merry flock of children.

But, impressed by their surroundings, the children were not very merry, and Marjorie sat decorously on the back seat with Rosy Posy beside her, while King and Kitty sat facing them.

It was a lovely afternoon, and the park drives were crowded with vehicles of all sorts. Marjorie secretly thought carriage driving rather tame after motoring, but there was so much to look at that it was really desirable to go rather slowly.

As they passed the lake, Parker, the footman, turned around, and asked them if they would like to get out and see the swans.

They welcomed this opportunity, and the footman gravely assisted them from the carriage. He selected a bench for them, and the four sat down upon it without a word.

At last the funny side of the situation struck King, and as he looked at his three demure sisters, he couldn't stand it another minute. "I'll race you down to that big tree," he whispered to Marjorie, and like a flash the two were off, with their; heels flying out behind them.

Parker was scandalized at this performance, but he said nothing, and only looked at Kitty and Rosamond, still sitting demurely on the bench.

"They'll come back in a minute," said Kitty, and the footman answered respectfully, "Yes, Miss."

"Did you ever see anything like it?" said King to Marjorie, as they reached the big tree almost at the same time.

"It's awful funny," Midget returned, "but just for a day or two, I don't mind it. It's such a new experience that it's rather fun. Only it's such a temptation to shock Grandpa and Grandma Maynard. I feel like doing something crazy just to see what they would do. But we promised not to get into any mischief. Shall we go back now?"

"Might as well; if we stay much longer it will be mischief. I'll race you back to the carriage."

Back they flew as fast as they had come, and when they reached the others, their cheeks were glowing and their eyes sparkling with the exercise.

The impassive footman made no comments, and in fact, he said nothing at all, but stood like a statue with the carriage robe over his arm.

So Marjorie assumed command, and said quietly, "We will go back now, Parker," and the man said, "Yes, ma'am," and touched his hat, quite as if she had been Grandma Maynard herself.

But the very fact of being in a position of responsibility made Marjorie more audacious, and as the man put them into the carriage, she said, "On the way home, we will stop somewhere for soda water."

"Yes, ma'am," replied Parker, and he took his place on the box.

The others looked at Marjorie a little doubtfully, but greatly pleased at the suggestion. And after all it certainly was not mischievous to get soda water, a treat which they were often allowed at home.

They left the park, and drove down Fifth Avenue, and after a while the carriage stopped in front of a large drug shop.

Parker assisted them from the carriage, and ushered them into the shop, which had a well-appointed soda fountain. Then Parker proceeded to select four seats for his charges, and after he had lifted Rosamond up on to her stool, and the rest were seated, he said to Marjorie, "Will you give the order, Miss Maynard?"

Feeling very grownup, Marjorie asked the others what flavors they would like, and then she gave the order to the clerk. The footman stood behind them, grave and impassive, and as there was a large mirror directly in front of them, Marjorie could see him all the time. It struck her very funny to see the four Maynards eating their ice cream soda, without laughing or chatting, and with a statuesque footman in charge of them! However, the Maynards' enjoyment of their favorite dainty was not seriously marred by the conditions, and when at last they laid down their spoons, Marjorie suddenly realized that she had no money with her to pay for their treat.

"Have you any money, King?" she asked.

"Not a cent; I never dreamed of having any occasion to use it, and I didn't bring any with me."

"What shall we do?" said Kitty, who foresaw an embarrassing situation.

"If you have finished, I will pay the check," said Parker, "and then, are you ready to go home, Miss Maynard?"

"Yes, thank you," said Marjorie, delighted to be relieved from her anxiety about the money.

So Parker paid the cashier, and then marshalled his charges out of the shop, and in a moment they were once again on their way home.

"Pretty good soda water," said Marjorie.

"Yes; but you might as well drink it in church," said King, who was beginning to tire of the atmosphere of restraint.

"I wish they did serve soda water in church," said Kitty; "it would be very refreshing."

And then they were back again at Grandpa Maynard's, and were admitted with more footmen and formality.

But Marjorie, with her adaptable nature, was beginning to get used to conventional observances, and, followed by the other three, she entered the drawing-room, and went straight to her Grandmother. "We had a very pleasant drive, thank you," she said, and her pretty, graceful manner brought a smile of approbation to her grandmother's face.

"I'm glad you did, my dear. Where did you go?"

"We drove in the park, and along the avenue," said King, uncertain whether to mention the soda water episode or not.

But Marjorie's frankness impelled her to tell the story, "We stopped at a drug shop, Grandma, on our way home, and had soda water," she said; "I hope you don't mind."

"You stopped at a drug shop!" exclaimed Grandma Maynard. "You four children alone!"

"We weren't alone," explained Marjorie "Parker went in with us, and he paid for it. Wasn't it all right, Grandma?"

"No; children ought not to go in a shop without older people with them."

"But Parker is older than we are," said Kitty, who was of a literal nature.

"Don't be impertinent, Kitty," said her grandmother. "I do not refer to servants."

Now Kitty had not had the slightest intention of being impertinent, and so the reproof seemed a little unfair.

Unable to control her indignation, when she saw Kitty's feelings were hurt, Marjorie tried to justify her sister.

"Kitty didn't mean that for impertinence, Grandma Maynard," she said. "We didn't know it wasn't right to go for soda water alone, for we always do it at home. The only thing that bothered me was because I didn't have the money to pay for it."

"The money is of no consequence, child; and I suppose you do not know that in the city, children cannot do quite the same as where you live. However, we will say no more about the matter."

64

This was a satisfactory termination of the subject, but Grandma's manner was not pleasant, and the children felt decidedly uncomfortable.

Their own parents had listened to the discussion in silence, but now their father said, "Don't be too hard on them, Mother; they didn't mean to do anything wrong. And they are good children, if not very conventional ones."

But Grandma Maynard only said, "We need not refer to the matter again," and then she told the children to go to their supper, which was ready for them.

As the four sat down to a prettily-appointed table, they were not a happy looking crowd. Rosamond was too young to understand what it was all about, but she knew that the other three were depressed and that was a very unusual state of things.

"I don't want any supper," began Kitty, but this speech was too much for King. Kitty was very fond of good things to eat, and for her to lose her appetite was comical indeed!

A pleasant-faced maid waited on them, and when Kitty saw the creamed sweet-breads and fresh peas and asparagus, with delightful little tea biscuits, her drooping spirits revived, and she quite forgot that Grandma had spoken sharply to her.

"You're all right, Kit," said King, approvingly. "I was frightened when you said you had lost your appetite, but I guess it was a false alarm."

"It was," said Kitty. "I do love sweet-breads."

"And there's custard pudding to come, Miss Kitty," said the maid, who smiled kindly on the children. In fact, she smiled so kindly that they all began to feel more cheerful, and soon were laughing and chatting quite in their usual way.

"What is your name, please?" inquired Marjorie, and the maid answered, "Perkins."
"Well, Perkins, do you know what we are to do to-morrow? Has Grandma made any plans for us?"

"Oh, yes, Miss Marjorie; she made the plans some weeks ago, as soon as she heard you were coming. She is giving a children's party for you to-morrow afternoon."

"A children's party! How kind of her!" And Marjorie quite forgot Grandma's disapproving remarks about the soda water escapade.
"Oh, I don't know," said King. "I expect a children's party here will be rather grownuppish."

"Oh, no, Master King," said Perkins; "there are only children invited. Young boys and girls of your own age. I'm sure it will be a very nice party."

"I'm sure of it, too," said Marjorie, "and I think it was awfully good of her, as we're to be here such a short time."

"Well, she needn't have said I was impertinent, when I wasn't," said Kitty, who still felt aggrieved at the recollection.

"Oh, never mind that, Kit," said good-natured Marjorie. "As long as you didn't mean to be, it doesn't really matter."

When the supper was over, Rosamond was sent to bed, and the other three were allowed to sit in the library for an hour. The ladies were dressing for dinner, but Grandpa Maynard came in and talked to them for a while.

At first they were all very grave and formal, but by a lucky chance, King hit upon a subject that recalled Grandpa's boyish days, and the old gentleman chuckled at the recollection.

"Tell us something about when you were a boy," said Marjorie. "I do believe, Grandpa, you were fond of mischief!"

"I was!" and Grandpa Maynard smiled genially. "I believe I got into more scrapes than any boy in school!"

"Then that's where we inherited it," said Marjorie. "I've often wondered why we were so full of capers. Was Father mischievous when he was a boy?"

"Yes, he was. He used to drive his mother nearly crazy by the antics he cut up. And he was always getting into danger. He would climb the highest trees, and swim in the deepest pools; he was never satisfied to let any other boy get ahead of him."

"That accounts for his being such a successful man," said King.

"Yes, perhaps it does, my boy. He was energetic and persistent and ambitious, and those qualities have stood by him all his life."

"But, Grandpa," said Marjorie, who had suddenly begun to feel more confidential with her grandfather, "why, then, do you and Grandma want us children to be so sedate and poky and quiet and good? At home we're awfully noisy, and here if we make a breath of noise we get reprimanded!"

"Well, you see, Marjorie, Grandma and I are not as young as we were, and we're so unused now to having children about us, that I dare say we do expect them to act like grown people. And, too, your grandmother is of a very formal nature, and she requires correct behavior from everybody. So I hope you will try your best while you're here not to annoy her."

"Indeed, we will try, Grandpa," said Marjorie. "I think she's very kind to make a party for us to-morrow, and I'm sure we ought to behave ourselves. But, Grandpa, you don't know what it is to have to sit so stiff and still when you're accustomed to racing around and yelling."

"Yes, I suppose that is so; though I didn't know that you were noisy children. Now I'll tell you what you can do. You can go up in the big billiard room on the top floor of the house,

66

and there you can make all the noise you like. You can play games or tell stories or do whatever you choose."

"Oh! that's lovely, Grandpa," and Marjorie threw her arms around his neck. "And won't anybody hear us if we make an awful racket?"

"No, the room is too far distant. Now run along up there, and you can have a pillow-fight if you want to. I believe that's what children enjoy."

"Well, you come with us, Grandpa, and show us the way," said Kitty, slipping her hand in his.

And with Marjorie on the other side, and King close behind, they all went upstairs. The billiard room, though not now used for its original purpose, was large and pleasant. There was not much furniture in it, but a cushioned seat ran nearly all round the room with many pillows on it. As soon as they were fairly in the room, Marjorie picked up a soft and fluffy pillow, and tossed it at her grandfather, hitting him squarely in the back of the neck.

The others were a little frightened at Marjorie's audacity, and Grandpa Maynard himself was startled as the pillow hit him. But as he turned and saw Marjorie's laughing face, he entered into the spirit of the game, and in a moment pillows were flying among the four, and shouts of merriment accompanied the fun.

Grandpa Maynard took off his glasses, and put them in his pocket for safekeeping, and soon he was the merriest one of all.

But suddenly he recollected that it was time for him to attend to his own duties as host.

"You young rascals," he said, "I don't know how you inveigled me into this disgraceful performance! Here I am all dishevelled, and in a few moments I must preside at dinner!"

"Oh, you're all right," said Marjorie, patting his necktie; "just brush your hair over again, and put your glasses on, and you'll look fine. And we're much obliged to you, Grandpa, for playing so jolly with us."

"Well, well; I'm surprised at myself! But remember this kind of play is only to be indulged in when you're up here. When you're downstairs, you must be polite and quiet-mannered, or else Grandma won't be pleased."

"All right," said Marjorie. "We promise we will," and all the others agreed.

CHAPTER XIII
A CHILDREN'S PARTY
The next day the children tried very hard to be good. It was not easy, for Grandma seemed especially punctilious, and reprimanded them for every little thing. She told them of the party in the afternoon, and taught them how to make curtseys to greet the guests.

"I know how to curtsey," said Marjorie. "I always do it at home, when mother has callers. But I don't curtsey to children."

"Yes, you must," said Grandma. "I don't want my grandchildren behaving like a lot of rustics."

This speech greatly offended Marjorie, and it was with difficulty that she refrained from answering that they were not rustics. But she controlled herself, and said that of course she would curtsey to the young guests if Grandma wished her to.

"Now that's a little lady," said Grandma, approvingly, and Marjorie felt glad that she hadn't given way to her irritation.

"What time is the party, Grandma?" asked Kitty.

"From four to six, Kitty; but you children must be dressed, and in the drawing-room at quarter before four."

The day dragged along, as there was nothing especial to do and no way to have any fun. Grandpa Maynard had gone out with their father, and though the children went up in the billiard room they didn't feel just like romping.

"I hate this house!" said King, unable to repress the truth any longer.

"So do I!" said Kitty. "If we stay here much longer, I'll run away."

This surprised the other two, for Kitty was usually mild and gentle, and rarely gave way to such speech as this.

"It's Grandma Maynard that makes the trouble," said King. "She's so pernickety and fussy about us. I'd behave a great deal better if she'd let me alone. And Grandpa wouldn't bother about us if Grandma didn't make him."

"I don't think you ought to talk like that, King," said Marjorie. "Somehow, it doesn't seem right. It isn't respectful, and all that, and it doesn't seem a nice thing to do."

"That's so, Mops; you're just right!" said King, taking the reproof in good part, for he knew it was merited. "It's a whole lot worse to be disrespectful about your grandpeople than to carry on and make a racket, I think."

"Yes, it is," said Marjorie, "and I say the rest of the time we're here, let's try to do just right. Because it's only two or three days anyway. I think we're going on day after to-morrow."

So they all agreed to try afresh to behave correctly, and on the whole succeeded pretty well.

Promptly at quarter of four that afternoon they presented themselves in the drawing-room for Grandma's inspection.

"You look very well," Grandma said, nodding her head approvingly at the girls' frilly white dresses and King's correct clothes. "Now I trust you'll behave as well as you look."

"What do you want us to do, Grandma?" asked Marjorie. "I mean to entertain the boys and girls."

"Oh, nothing of that sort, child; the entertainment will be provided by a professional entertainer. You have only to greet the guests properly, and that is all you need do."

Marjorie did not know quite what a professional entertainer was, but it sounded interesting, and she was quite sure she could manage to greet the guests politely.

Although Marjorie's mother was in the room, she had little to say, for Grandma Maynard was accustomed to dominate everything in her own house. And as her ideas were not entirely in accord with those of her daughter-in-law, the younger Mrs. Maynard thought it wise not to obtrude her own opinions.

Promptly at four o'clock the children began to come. The Maynards stood in a group at one end of the long room, and as each guest arrived, a footman stationed at the doorway announced the name in a loud voice. Then each little guest came and curtsied to the receiving party, and after a few polite remarks, passed on, and was ushered to a seat by another footman.

The seats were small, gilt chairs with red cushions, arranged all round the wall, and there were about forty.

In a short time the guests were all in their places, and then the Maynards were shown to their seats.
Then the professional entertainer arrived. She proved to be a pretty and pleasant young lady, and she wore a light blue satin gown and a pink rose in her hair.

First, she sang a song for them, and then she told a story, and then she recited a poem.

Then she asked the children what they would like to have next. At first no one responded, and then a little girl said, "Won't you sing us another song, please. You sing so delightfully."

Marjorie looked in amazement at the child who talked in such grownup fashion. But the entertaining lady did not seem to think it strange, and she replied, "Yes, I will sing for you with pleasure."

So she sang another song, but though it was pretty music, Marjorie could not understand the words, and she began to think that the programme was rather tiresome.

The lady kept on telling stories and reciting poems, and singing, until Marjorie almost had the fidgets. It seemed so unlike her notion of a children's party, to sit still and listen to a programme all the afternoon, and she grew cramped and tired, and longed for it to be over. But the city children did not seem to feel that way at all. They sat very demurely with their hands clasped, and their slippered feet crossed, and applauded politely at the proper times.

Marjorie glanced at King and Kitty, and their answering glances proved that they felt exactly as she did herself. However, all three were determined to do the right thing, and so they sat still, and tried to look as if they were enjoying themselves.

At half-past five the programme came to an end, and the children were invited to go out into the dining-room for the feast.

The dining-room was transformed into a place of beauty. Small tables accommodated six guests each, and at each place was a lovely basket of flowers with a big bow of gauze ribbon on the handle. Each table had a different color, and the flowers in the basket matched the ribbon bow. Marjorie's basket was filled with pink sweet peas, while at another table Kitty had lavender pansies, and King found himself in front of a basket of yellow daisies.

The feast, as might have been expected at Grandma Maynard's, was delicious, but the Maynard children could not enjoy it very much because of their environment. They were not together, and each one being with several strangers, felt it necessary to make polite conversation.

King tried to talk on some interesting subject to the little girl who sat next him.

"Have you a flower garden?" he said.

"Oh, no, indeed; we live in the city, so we can't very well have a flower garden."

"No, of course not," agreed King. "You see, we live in the country, so we have lots of flowers."

"It must be dreadful to live in the country," commented the little girl, with a look of scorn.

"It isn't dreadful at all," returned King; "and just now, in springtime, it's lovely. The flowers are all coming out, and the birds are hopping around, and the grass is getting green. What makes you say it's dreadful?"

"Oh, I don't like the country," said the child, with a shrug of her little shoulders. "The grass is wet, and there aren't any pavements, and everything is so disagreeable."

"You're thinking of a farm; I don't mean that kind of country," and then King remembered that he ought not to argue the question, but agree with the little lady, so he said, "But of course if you don't like the country, why you don't, that's all"

"Yes, that's all," said the little girl, and then the conversation languished, for the children seemed to have no subjects in common.

At her table, Marjorie was having an equally difficult time. There was a good-looking and pleasant-faced boy sitting next to her, so she said, "Do you have a club?"

"Oh, no," returned the boy; "my father belongs to clubs, but I'm too young."

"But I don't mean that kind," explained Marjorie; "I mean a club just for fun. We have a Jinks Club,—we cut up jinks, you know."

"How curious!" said the boy. "What are jinks?"

Marjorie thought the boy rather silly not to know what jinks were, for she thought any one with common sense ought to know that, but she said, "Why, jinks are capers,—mischief,— any kind of cutting up."

"And you have a club for that?" exclaimed the boy, politely surprised.

"Yes, we do," said Marjorie, determined to stand up for her own club. "And we have lovely times. We do cut up jinks, but we try to make them good jinks, and we play all over the house, and out of doors, and everywhere."

"It must be great fun," said the boy, but he said it in such an uninterested tone that Marjorie gave up talking to him, and turned her attention to the neighbor on her other side.

When the supper was over, the young guests all took their leave. Again the Maynards stood in a group to receive the good-byes, and every child expressed thanks for the afternoon's pleasure in a formal phrase, and curtsied, and went away.

When they had all gone, the Maynard children looked at each other, wondering what to do next.

"You may go up to the billiard room and play, if you like," said Grandma, benignly. "You will not want any other supper to-night, I'm sure; so you may play up there until bedtime."

Rosy Posy was carried away by the nurse, but the three other children started for the billiard room. Marjorie, however, turned back to say, "We all thank you, Grandma Maynard, for the party you gave us."

Kitty and King murmured some sort of phrase that meant about the same thing, but as they had not enjoyed the party at all they didn't make their thanks very effusive, and then the three walked decorously upstairs. But once inside the billiard room, with the door shut, they expressed their opinions.

"That was a high old party, wasn't it?" said King.

"The very worst ever!" declared Kitty. "I never got so tired of anything in my life, as I did listening to that entertaining person, or whatever they call her."

"It was an awful poky party," said Marjorie, "but I think we ought to give Grandma credit for meaning to give us pleasure. Of course she's used to children who act like that, and she couldn't even imagine the kind of parties we have at home, where we frolic around and have a good time. So I say don't let's jump on her party, but remember that she did it for us, and she did it the best she knew how."

"You're a good sort, Mopsy," said King, looking at his sister affectionately. "What you say is all right, and it goes. Now let's cut out that party and try to forget it."

There were some quiet games provided for the children, and so they played parcheesi and authors until bedtime, for though the billiard room was hardly within hearing of their grandparents, yet they did not feel like playing romping games.

"I don't think I shall ever holler again," said King. "I'm getting so accustomed to holding my breath for fear I'll make too much noise that I'll probably always do so after this."

"No, you won't," said practical Kitty. "As soon as you get away from Grandma Maynard's house you'll yell like a wild Indian."
"I expect I will," agreed King. "Come on, let's play Indians now."

"Nope," said Marjorie; "we'd get too noisy, and make mischief. I'm going to bed; I'm awfully tired."

"So'm I," said Kitty. "Parties like that are enough to wear anybody out!"

They all went downstairs to their bedrooms, but as Marjorie passed the door of her grandmother's room, she paused and looked in.

"May I come in, Grandma?" she said. "I do love to see you in your beautiful clothes. You look just lovely."

Marjorie's compliment was very sincere, for she greatly admired her grandmother, and in spite of her formality, and even severity, Marjorie had a good deal of affection for her.

The maid was just putting the finishing touches to Mrs. Maynard's costume, and as she stood; robed in mauve satin, with sparkling diamond ornaments, she made a handsome picture. Mrs. Maynard was a beautiful woman, and exceedingly young-looking for her age. There was scarcely a thread of gray in her dark brown hair, and the natural roses still bloomed on her soft cheeks.

Marjorie had not seen her grandmother before in full evening attire, and she walked round, gazing at her admiringly.

"I don't wonder my father is such a handsome man," she said. "He looks ever so much like you."

Grandma Maynard was pleased at this naïve compliment, for she knew Marjorie was straightforward and sincere. She smiled at her little granddaughter, saying, "I'm glad you're pleased with your family's personal appearance, and I think some day you will grow up to be a pretty young lady yourself; but you must try to remember that handsome is as handsome does."

Marjorie's adaptable nature quickly took color from her surroundings and influences, and gazing at her refined and dignified grandmother, she said earnestly, "When I grow up,

Grandma, I hope I'll look just like you, and I hope I'll behave just like you. I am rather a naughty little girl; but you see I was born just chock-full of mischief, and I can't seem to get over it."

"You are full of mischief, Marjorie, but I think you will outgrow it. Why, if you lived with me, I believe you'd turn my hair white in a single night."

"That would be a pity, Grandma," and Marjorie smiled at the carefully waved brown locks which crowned her grandma's forehead.

"Now I'm going down to dinner, Marjorie,—we have guests coming. But if you like, you may amuse yourself for a little while looking round this room. In that treasure cabinet are many pretty curios, and I know I can trust you to be careful of my things."

"Thank you, Grandma; I will look about here for a little while, and indeed I will be careful not to harm anything."

So Grandma's satin gown rustled daintily down the stairs, and Marjorie was left alone in her beautifully appointed bedroom.

She opened the treasure cabinet, and spent a pleasant half hour looking over the pretty things it contained. She was a careful child, and touched the things daintily, putting each back in its right place after she examined it.

Then she locked the glass doors of the cabinet, and walked leisurely about the room, looking at the pretty furnishings. The dainty toilet table interested her especialty, and she admired its various appointments, some of which she did not even know the use of. One beautiful carved silver affair she investigated curiously, when she discovered it was a powder box, which shook out scented powder from a perforated top. Marjorie amused herself, shaking some powder on her hand, and flicking it on her rosy cheeks. It was a fascinating little affair, for it worked by an unusual sort of a spring, and Marjorie liked to play with it.

She wandered about the room with the powder-box still in her hand, and as she paused a moment at Grandma's bedside, a brilliant idea came to her.

The bed had been arranged for the night. The maid had laid aside the elaborate lace coverlet and pillow covers, had deftly turned back the bed clothing in correct fashion, and had put Grandma's night pillow in place.

For some reason, as Marjorie looked at the pillow, there flashed across her mind what Grandma had said about her hair turning white in a single night, and acting on a sudden impulse, Marjorie shook powder from the silver box all over Grandma's pillow. Then chuckling to herself, she replaced the powder-box on the dressing table, and went to her own room.

CHAPTER XIV
A MERRY JOKE

The next morning, while Marjorie was dressing, she heard a great commotion in the halls. Peeping out her door she saw maids running hither and thither with anxious, worried faces. She heard her grandmother's voice in troubled accents, and Grandfather seemed to be trying to soothe her.

Naughty Marjorie well knew what it was all about, and chuckled with glee as she finished dressing, and went down to breakfast.

She found the family assembled in the breakfast room, and Grandma Maynard telling the story. "Yes," she said, "I knew perfectly well that to have these children in the house, with their noise and racket, would so get on my nerves that it would turn my hair white, and it has done so!"

Marjorie looked at Grandma Maynard's hair, and though not entirely white, it was evenly gray all over. As she had laid her head on her plentifully-powdered pillow, and perhaps restlessly moved it about, the powder had distributed itself pretty evenly, and the result was a head of gray hair instead of the rich brown tresses of the night before.

Her son and daughter-in-law could not believe that this effect was caused by the disturbance made by their own children; but far less did they suspect the truth of the matter. Whatever opinions the various members of the family held as to the cause of the phenomenon, not one of them suspected Marjorie's hand in the matter.

As for Midget herself, she was convulsed with glee, although she did not show it. Never had she played a joke which had turned out so amazingly well, and the very fact that neither Kitty nor King knew anything about it lessened the danger of detection.

"It seems incredible," Grandma went on, "that this thing should really happen to me, for I've so often feared it might; and then to think it should come because the visit of my own grandchildren was so upsetting to my nerves!"

"Nonsense, Mother," said her son, "it couldn't have been that! It isn't possible that the children, no matter how much they carried on, would have any such effect as that!"

"You may say so, Ed; but look at the effect, and then judge for yourself; what is your explanation of this disaster that has come to me?"

"I don't know, I'm sure, Mother,—but it couldn't be what you suggest.
I've heard of such an accident happening to people, but I never believed
it before. Now I'm forced to admit it must be true. What do you think,
Helen?"
Mrs. Maynard looked thoughtful. "I don't know," she said slowly, "but it must be the symptom of some disease or illness that has suddenly attacked Mother Maynard."

"But I'm perfectly well," declared the older lady; "and a thing like this doesn't happen without some reason; and there's no reason for it, except some great mental disturbance, and I've had nothing of that sort except the visit of these children! Ed, you'll have to take them away."

"I think I shall have to," said Mr. Maynard, gravely. It was a great trial to him that his parents could not look more leniently upon his children. He had rarely brought them to visit their grandparents, because it always made his mother nervous and irritable. But it was too absurd to think that such nervousness and irritation could cause her brown hair to turn almost white, a proceeding which he had always thought was a mere figure of speech anyway.

Breakfast proceeded in an uncomfortable silence. It was useless to try to console Grandma Maynard, or to make her think that the gray hair was becoming to her. Indeed, everything that was said only made her more disconsolate about the fate which had overtaken her, and more annoyed at the children, whom she considered to blame.

At last, sharp-eyed, practical Kitty volunteered the solution. She had sat for some time watching her grandmother, and at last she felt sure that she saw grains of powder fall from the gray hair to the shoulder of Grandma's gown. When she was fully convinced that this was the case, she looked straight at the victim of misfortune and said, "Grandma, I think you are playing a trick on us. I think you have powdered your hair, and you are only pretending it has turned gray."

"What do you mean, Kitty, child?" said her father, in amazement, for it almost seemed as if Kitty were rebuking her grandmother.

"Why, just look, Father! There is powder shaking down on Grandma's shoulder."

"Nonsense!" cried Grandma, angrily. "I'd be likely to do a thing like that, wouldn't I, Miss Kitty? And indeed, if it were powder, and could be brushed out, and leave my hair its natural color, I should be only too grateful!"

This was Marjorie's chance. She loved to make a sensation, and laying down her knife and fork, she said, quietly, "Kitty is right, Grandma; it is nothing but powder, and I put it there myself."

"What!" exclaimed Grandma. "Do you mean to say, Marjorie, that you powdered my hair? How did you do it? Oh, child, if you are telling me the truth, if it is really only powder, I shall be so relieved that I will make you a handsome present!"

This was a new turn of affairs, indeed! Marjorie had had misgivings as to the results of her practical joke, but it had seemed to her merely a harmless jest, and she had hoped that it might be taken lightly. But when Grandma expressed such consternation at her whitened hair, Marjorie had been shaking in her shoes, lest she should be punished, rather than laughed at for her trick. And now to be offered a beautiful present was astonishing, truly! The ways of grownups were surely not to be counted upon!

With lightened spirits, then, and with sparkling eyes, Marjorie completed her confession. "Yes," she went on, "after you said last night that you b'lieved us children could turn your hair white in a single night, I thought I'd make believe we did. So,—and you know, Grandma, you told me I could stay around in your room for a while, and look at your pretty things,— so, when I saw that queer sort of a powder-shaker I couldn't help playing with it. And then when I saw your bed all fixed so nice for the night, I thought it would be fun to powder your

75

pillow. I've heard of people doing it before. I didn't make it up myself. So I shook the powder all over your pillow, and then of course you put your head on it, and of course it made your hair white."

Marjorie's parents looked aghast, for to them it seemed as if she had simply played a practical joke on her grandmother, and one not easily forgiven, but Grandpa Maynard expressed himself in a series of chuckles.

"Chip of the old block," he said. "Chip of the old block! Just what you would have done, Ed, when you were a boy, if you had thought of it! Marjorie, practical jokes run in the family, and you can't help your propensity for them! I don't approve of them, mind you, I don't approve of them, but once in a while when one works out so perfectly, I can't help enjoying it. What do you say, Mother?"

He turned to his wife, and to the surprise of all, she was beaming with joy. It was not so much her enjoyment of the joke as her relief at finding that her hair had not turned gray, and could easily be restored to its beautiful brown.

"I'm quite sure I ought to be annoyed," she said, smiling at Marjorie. "I'm almost certain I ought to be very angry, and I know you ought to be punished. But none of these things are going to happen. I'm so glad that it is only a joke that I forgive the little jokemaker, and as I promised, I will give you a present as an expression of my gratitude."

And so the breakfast ended amid general hilarity, and afterward Grandma took Marjorie up to her own room, and they had a little quiet talk.

"I don't want you to misunderstand me, dear," she said, "for practical jokes are not liked by most people, and they're not a nice amusement for a little girl. But, I'm afraid, Marjorie, that I have been too harsh and stern with you, and so I think we can even things up this way. I will pass over the rudeness and impertinence of your deed, if you will promise me not to make a practice of such jokes throughout your life. Or at least, we will say, on older people. I suppose a good-natured joke on your schoolfellows now and then does no real harm; but I want you to promise me never again to play such a trick on your elders."

"I do promise, Grandma; and I want to tell you that your kindness to me makes me feel more ashamed of my naughty trick than if you had punished me. You see, Grandma, I do these things without thinking,—I mean without thinking hard enough. When the notion flies into my head it seems so funny that I just have to go on and do it! But I am trying to improve, and I don't cut up as many jinks as I used to."

"That's a good girl. Marjorie, I believe you'll make a fine woman, and I wish I could have the training of you. How would you like to come and live with me?"

"That's funny, Grandma," said Midget, laughing, "after all you've said about your not wanting us children in the house."

"I know it; and I can't stand the whole lot of you at once, but I really do believe, Marjorie, that I'll take you and bring you up. I shall speak to your father and mother about it at once."

"Oh, Grandma, don't!" And Marjorie clasped her hands, with a look of horror on her face. "Don't ask me to leave Mother and Father! And King, and Kitty, and the baby! Why, Grandma, I couldn't do it, any more than I could fly!"

"Why not? You don't realize all I could do for you. We live much more handsomely than you do at home, and I would give you everything you wanted."

"But, Grandma, all those things wouldn't make any difference if I had to leave my dear people! Why, do you really s'pose I'd even think of such a thing! Why, I couldn't live without my own father and mother! I love you and Grandpa, and since you've been so kind and forgiving this morning, I love you a lot more than I did; but, my goodness, gracious, sakes, I'd never live with anybody but my own special particular bunch of Maynards!"

"It's a question you can't decide for yourself, child. I shall speak to your parents about it, and they will appreciate better than you do the advantages it would mean for you to follow out my plan. Now I will give you the present I promised you, and I think it will be this very same silver powder-box. You probably do not use powder, but it is a pretty ornament to set on your dressing table, and I want you to let it remind you of your promise not to play practical jokes."

"Oh, thank you, Grandma," said Marjorie, as she took the pretty trinket; "I'm glad to have it, because it is so pretty. And I will remember my promise, and somehow I feel sure I'm going to keep it."

"I think you will, dear, and now you may run away for the present, as I am going to be busy."

Marjorie found King and Kitty in the billiard room, waiting for her.

"Well, you are the limit!" exclaimed King. "How did you ever dare cut up that trick, Mops? You got out of it pretty lucky, but I trembled in my boots at first. I don't see how you dared play a joke on Grandma Maynard of all people!"

"Why didn't you tell us about it?" asked Kitty. "Oh, did she give you that lovely powder-box?"

"Yes," laughed Marjorie, "as a reward for being naughty! And she's going to reward me further. What do you think? She's going to take me to live with her!"

"What!" cried King and Kitty, in the same breath. And then King grasped Marjorie by the arm. "You shan't go!" he cried. "I won't let you!"
"I won't either!" cried Kitty, grasping her other arm. "Why, Mops, we simply couldn't live without you!"

"I know it, you old goosey! And I couldn't live without you! The idea! As if any of us four Maynards could get along without any of each other!"

"I just guess we couldn't!" exclaimed King, and then as far as the children were concerned, the subject was dropped.

CHAPTER XV
A RIDE IN MAY
At the breakfast table, the next morning, Grandma Maynard announced her intention of keeping her oldest grandchild with her as her own.

Marjorie's mother looked up with a frightened glance at this declaration, and she turned her face appealingly toward her husband. But when she saw the twinkle in his eye, she knew at once there was not the slightest danger of her losing her oldest daughter in this way.

But, apparently by way of a joke, Mr. Maynard saw fit to pretend to approve of his mother's plan.

"Why, Mother," he said, "wouldn't that be fine! This big house needs a young person in it, and as we have four, we ought to be able to spare one. You'll have grand times, Midget, living here, won't you?"

If Marjorie had not been so overcome at the very thought of leaving her own family, she would have realized that her father was only joking; but she had been so truly afraid that her grandmother's wishes might possibly be granted that she couldn't realize her father's intent.

"Oh, Father!" she cried, with a perfect wail of woe; and then, jumping from her seat at the table, she ran to her mother's side, and flung herself into her arms, where she gave way to one of her tumultuous crying spells.

Poor little Marjorie was not greatly to blame. She had lain awake the night before, fearing that this thing might happen, and so was in no mood to appreciate a jest on the subject.

Unwilling to have such a commotion at the breakfast table, Mrs. Maynard rose, and with her arm round the sobbing child, drew her away to an adjoining room, where she reassured her fears, and told her that her father did not at all mean what he had said.

"Now, you see, Mother," Mr. Maynard went on, "how Midget feels about the matter. Well, my feelings are exactly the same, only I choose a different mode of expression. I'm sorry the child is so upset because I jokingly agreed to the plan, but she'll get over it in a few minutes, with her mother's help. And as you must know, Mother, we appreciate how fine it would be for Marjorie to live here, and be the petted darling of you two dear people, but you must also know that it is just as much out of the question for us to give you one of our children as it would be to give you the whole four!"

"That's a gift I wouldn't care for," said Grandma Maynard, smiling at the other three; "but I have taken a great fancy to Marjorie, and I know I could make her love me."

At this moment Marjorie and her mother returned, both with smiling, happy faces. Marjorie heard her grandmother's last words, and running to her, she threw her arms around the old lady's neck.

"I do love you, Grandma," she cried, "but of course you must know that I couldn't leave my own Maynards. Why, we're the 'votedest family you ever did see! We couldn't spare any one of each other! And, Grandma, when you were a little girl twelve years old, you wouldn't have gone away from your father and mother to live, would you?"

"No, Marjorie, I don't suppose I would," admitted Grandma Maynard, patting the little girl's cheek; "but perhaps when you're older, dear, you may change your mind about this."

Marjorie looked thoughtful a moment, and then she said, "Grandma, I don't truly think I will, but if I should I'll let you know."

"I hadn't an idea the child would come to live with us," said Grandpa Maynard, "but how's this for a suggestion? Let her come to visit us for a time every year. I believe she makes long visits to her other grandmother."

Marjorie smiled involuntarily at the thought of the difference between the homes of the two grandmothers, but she said nothing, knowing from what her mother had told her that she would not be sent away from home unless she chose.

"Oh, Midget doesn't visit Grandma Sherwood every year," said Marjorie's father. "She only goes there once in four years. So to even matters up, suppose we let Marjorie come here and make a little visit next winter, with the understanding that if she gets homesick, she's to be sent home at once."

Everybody agreed to this, and though Marjorie felt a positive conviction that she would get homesick about the second day, yet Grandma Maynard made a silent resolve that she would make everything so attractive to Marjorie that the visit would be a long one.

So the matter was settled for the present, and if King and Kitty felt a little chagrined at Grandma Maynard's preference for Marjorie's company over their own, they said nothing about it.

* * * * *

That same afternoon, directly after luncheon, the Maynard family started once more on their automobile trip.

As the big car drew up in front of the house, the children saw it with joy, but they did not express their feelings, as that would not be polite to their grandparents.

But they were secretly delighted to see the big car again, with Pompton, whom they had not seen since they had been in New York, in his seat waiting for them.

Then good-byes were said, and Grandma affectionately reminded Marjorie that she was to visit her in the winter, and then in a few moments the motor party was speeding away.

They were scarcely a block from the house before the children began to express their relief at being released from the uncongenial atmosphere of their grandparents' home.

"I do declare," said King. "It was just like being in jail!"

"Have you ever been in jail?" asked Kitty, who was nothing if not literal.

"Well, no," returned her brother, "and I hope I never shall be after this experience. Grandpa and Grandma Maynard are the limit! If I had stayed there another day, I should have run away!"

Mr. Maynard, who was sitting in front with Pompton, turned round to the children.

"My dear little Maynards," he said, "unless you want to hurt your father's feelings very badly indeed, you will stop this severe criticism of your grandparents. You must remember that they are my father and mother, and that I love them very dearly, and I want you to do the same. If their ways don't suit you, remember that children should not criticise their elders, and say nothing about them. If there is anything about them that you do like, comment on that, but remain silent as to the things that displeased you."

The Maynard children well knew that when their father talked seriously like this, it was intended as a grave reproof, and they always took it so.

"Father," said King, manfully, "I was wrong to speak as I did, and I'm sorry, and I won't do it again. We didn't any of us like to be at Grandma Maynard's, but I was the only one who spoke so disrespectfully. Midge and Kitty were awfully nice about it."
"No, we weren't," confessed Kitty. "At least, I wasn't. Midget said lots of times that we oughtn't to be disrespectful, but I guess I was. But, you see, Father, it was awfully hard to please those people."

"We didn't understand them," said Marjorie, thoughtfully. "When I tried to be good I got scolded, and when I cut up jinks they gave me a present for it! Who could know what to do in a house like that?"

Mr. Maynard smiled in spite of himself.

"I think you've struck it, Midget," he said. "Grandma and Grandpa Maynard are a little inconsistent, and don't always know exactly what they do want. But that is largely because they are not very young, and they live alone, and are all unused to the vagaries of children. But these facts are to be accepted, not criticised, and I want you to remember, once for all, that you're not to say anything further disrespectful or unkind about your grandparents. And I think I know you well enough to know that you'll understand and obey these instructions without any more scolding on my part."

"We will, Fathery," said Midget, pounding on his arm with her little fists, by way of affectionate emphasis.

"Yes, we will!" agreed King, heartily. "And so now let's cut it out and have a good time."

And have a good time they did. Swiftly traversing the upper part of New York City, they continued along delightful roads; sometimes passing through towns, sometimes getting views of the shining waters of Long Island Sound, and sometimes travelling through the green, open country. Partly because of the repression of the past few days, and partly because of the exhilaration of the fresh spring air and the fast speeding motor, the four young Maynards were in a state of hilarity. They sang and they shouted and they laughed, and often they would grab each other with affectionate squeezes from sheer joy of living.

"I guess we couldn't let old Mopsy go out of this bunch!" exclaimed King, as with a clever agility he pulled off both Midget's hair-ribbons at once.

This called for retaliation, and in a flash, Marjorie tweaked off his necktie.

Nobody knew exactly the particular fun in this performance, for it only meant an immediate readjustment of the same ribbons, but it was a frequent occurrence, and usually passed unnoticed.

"And old Mopsy couldn't stay away from this bunch, either," returned Marjorie, in response to her brother's remark. "Why, if I just tried it, I'm sure it would kill me!"
"I'm sure so, too," agreed Kitty. "We just have to have each other all the time, we do! Oh, Mops, there are some marshmallows; mayn't we get some, Mother?"

Sure enough, the big pink blooms showed on the marshmallow bushes, and in a minute the children had scrambled out to get some.

It was a muddy performance, for marshmallows have a way of growing in very swampy places, but the little Maynards didn't mind that, or at least, they didn't stop to think whether they did or not. Splash and paddle they went into the mud, but they succeeded in getting several of the beautiful flowers, and returned with them in triumph.

"Those are fine specimens," said Mr. Maynard, "but I can't possibly let those six muddy shoes get into this car that Pompton keeps so beautifully clean! Would you mind walking on to New Haven?"

The three looked at their shoes, and discovered that they were simply loaded with mud. Even when wiped off on the grass, they presented a most untidy appearance.

But King came to his sisters' rescue.

"I'll tell you what," he said. "You girls take off your shoes as you get in, and I'll take off mine as I get in, and then I'll take some newspaper, and polish them all up."

This really was a good idea, and King worked diligently away until he had rubbed the muddy shoes into a fair state of civilization.

Mr. Maynard, as he often did, composed a song for the occasion, and after once hearing it, the children took up the strain and sang heartily:

"Old King Cole
Rubbed a muddy old sole
  And a muddy old sole rubbed he;
For he polished each shoe
Of his sisters two,
  And his own shoes, they made three!
Hurray, hurroo, hurree!
  And his own shoes, they made three!"

Mr. Maynard's doggerel was always highly appreciated by the children, and they sang the pleasing ditty over and over, while King rubbed away at the shoes in time to the chorus.

The sun was setting as they neared New Haven. The approach, along the shores of the beautiful harbor, was most picturesque, and both the children and their parents were impressed by the beauty of the scene. The setting sun turned the rippling water to gold, and the shipping loomed against the sky like a forest of bare tree-trunks.

"Oh," exclaimed Marjorie, clasping her hands, "isn't it lovely to go motor-carring with your own dear family, and see such beautiful landscapes on the river?"

"Your expressions are a little mixed," said her father, laughing, "but I quite agree with your sentiments. And, now, who is ready for a good dinner?"

"I am," declared Kitty, promptly; and they all laughed, for Kitty was always the first in the dining-room.

The automobile stopped in front of a large hotel which overlooked the College Green. While Mr. Maynard was engaging rooms, Mrs. Maynard and the children lingered on the veranda. The beautiful trees of the City of Elms waved high above their heads, and across the Green they could see the stately college buildings.

"Can we go over there?" asked King, who was interested, because he hoped, himself, some day to go to college.

"Not to-night," said his father, who had just rejoined the group; "to-morrow morning, King, we will all go through the college grounds and buildings. But now we will go to our rooms and freshen up a bit, and then we must get some dinner for our poor, famishing Kitty."

Kitty laughed good-naturedly, for she was used to jokes about her appetite, and didn't mind them a bit.

They went upstairs to a pleasant suite of rooms, one of which was for the use of Midge and Kitty.

"You must change your frocks for dinner," said Mrs. Maynard to the girls.

"The suitcases will be sent up, and you may put on your light challies."

So Marjorie and Kitty made their toilettes, stopping now and then for frantic expressions of joy and delight at the fun they were having; and soon, with ribbons freshly tied, and dainty house slippers, they were ready to go downstairs.

CHAPTER XVI
AT THE CIRCUS

The next morning the Maynard family visited Yale College.

As Mrs. Maynard had seen most of the buildings before, she only cared to visit the newest ones, and so she and Rosy Posy spent most of the time wandering about the grounds or sitting on the benches beneath the Elms. Marjorie and Kitty rambled about as they liked, sometimes going through the buildings with their father and King, and sometimes staying with Mrs. Maynard and the baby.

At luncheon time, Mr. Maynard asked the children what they would like best to do for an afternoon's amusement.

"Aren't we going on to Boston this afternoon?" asked Marjorie, in surprise.

"No," said her father, "it's a long trip, and so we'll start to-morrow morning. Now you children may choose what you'd like to do this afternoon, for your mother and I are going to call on some friends, and we don't want to take you with us."

"Well," said Marjorie, "I can't think of anything we could do in New Haven, unless you or Mother were with us; so I suppose we'll just stay here at the hotel, and,—"

"And cut up jinks," put in King.

Mr. Maynard smiled. "That's exactly what you would do if I left you here by yourselves! So what do you think of this plan? As we shall be gone all the afternoon, I think I will let Pompton take you four infants to the circus."

"Oh, goody, goody!" cried Marjorie. "That will be perfectly gorgeous!
King, won't it be fine to go to the circus?"
"Yes, indeed! And it's a big circus,—I saw the posters yesterday on our way here."

"There are lovely wild animals!" said Kitty, ecstatically. "I saw pictures of lions and tigers,— terrific ones!"

"Me loves tigers," commented Rosy Posy. "They eat peoples all up!"

"These don't," said Kitty. "They're trained ones, and they do tricks.
Why, the man who trains them puts his hand right in their mouths!"
"Ugh!" said Marjorie, with a shudder. "I don't like that part of it. I wish they didn't have the wild beasts. I like the people who swing on a long swing,—"

"Trapeze," said her father.

"Yes, a trapeze; and they swing and catch each other by the feet. Oh, I love to see them!"

"So do I," said Kitty. "I love it all,—but I love the tigers best."

"You must promise to behave yourselves," said Mrs. Maynard. "Marjorie, I shall put the baby in your especial care, though of course Pompton will look out for you all. And you must all obey him, and do exactly as he tells you."

"There isn't much obeying to do," said King. "We just sit on seats and watch the show, don't we?"

"Oh, we walk around and see the side-shows," said Marjorie.

"Whatever you do," said Mr. Maynard, "stay with Pompton, and do just as he tells you. He is a very intelligent man, and he will take care of you all right, and you must be kind and polite to him. Now scamper along and get ready."

The children were soon ready, and went gaily off with Pompton, waving good-byes to their parents, who stood on the hotel veranda.

They did not go in their own automobile, but in a trolley-car, and the four children seated themselves demurely, side by side, with Pompton at the end, next to Rosy Posy.

The ride was through a pleasant part of town, and on to the outskirts, where they soon came in sight of the circus tents.

Pompton ushered his charges through the entrance, and they found themselves in what seemed like a wilderness of tents, both large and small. As it was not yet time for the performance, they walked round, visiting the side-shows, and looking at the collection of "freaks," which is considered an important part of every circus.

"Mayn't we have some popcorn, Pomp?" asked Marjorie, as they passed a stand where that delectable refreshment was sold.

"Your ma said you were to have that after the show, Miss Marjorie. At least, that's how I understood it." Pompton always took the children's requests very seriously, and only granted them when he could do so conscientiously.

"Oh, she wouldn't care, whether we had it before or after," said King; "but I'll tell you what, Pomp, let's have half now and half after the show."

"Very well, Master King. I don't suppose it does make any great matter.
Will you have pink or white?"
"Both," said Kitty, who was authority on these matters; "and then we'll have pink lemonade."

"But you've just had your luncheon, Miss Kitty."

"That doesn't matter; this is a sort of dessert. And of course if we have popcorn, we must have lemonade. Popcorn is so choky."

So the children had their refreshment, and then it was time to go to see the performance.

Pompton took Rosy Posy in his arms, and the others following, they went into the big tent and were ushered to their places.

Mr. Maynard had told Pompton to take a box, as in the small enclosure it was easier to keep an eye on the children, and make sure they did nothing they ought not to. For the little Maynards were impulsive, and though Pompton was wise and sensible, he was not entirely accustomed to their mischievous ways.

"Isn't this fun!" exclaimed Marjorie, as the usher showed them the small wooden enclosure with six hard chairs in it.

"Perfectly splendid!" agreed Kitty. "And we can have this extra chair for our wraps and things."

So with great content they settled in their places to watch the circus.

It began, as circuses usually do, with the chariot races, and these were Marjorie's especial delight. She had been to the circus several times, and she always enjoyed the classic-looking ladies who drove tumultuous horses, while they stood in gorgeously painted but very rattle-te-bang chariots.

"I should think they'd fall out behind," commented Kitty.

"They would if the horses stopped suddenly," said King.

"No, they wouldn't," said Marjorie. "If the horses stopped, they'd pitch over the dashboard; but the horses aren't going to stop! Oh, there comes the blue one again! Isn't she a dandy? King, I'd love to drive one of those chariots!"

"Don't you try it on now. Miss Marjorie," said Pompton, on hearing this speech.

"Of course, I won't, Pomp," said Marjorie, laughing. "I only said I'd like to. Oh, now that's all over, and they're going to have the ladies and gentlemen who ride tip-toe on their horses. I think I like that next best to the trapeze people."

"I like it all," said contented little Kitty, whose nature it was to take things as they came.

Fascinated, they all watched the bare-back riding, and after that the acrobats, and then the trapeze performers.

"Wow! but they're wonders!" exclaimed King, as the trapezists swayed through the air, and caught flying rings or swings, and seemed every time to escape missing them only by a hairsbreadth. But they always caught them, and swung smilingly back, as if living up in the air were quite as pleasant as walking about on the ground.

"Oh, I'd like to do that!" cried Marjorie, as with sparkling eyes she watched a young girl do a swinging specialty.

King laughed. "You'd like to do lots of these stunts, Midget, but let me advise you if you're ever a circus performer, don't try trapeze work; you're too heavy. When you came down, you'd go smash through the net! If you must be in a circus, you'd better stick to your chariot driving."

"Now the trapeze number is over," said Kitty, looking at her programme, "and next will be the wild animals! I do love to see those."

"And I don't," said Marjorie, with a shudder. It was not exactly fear, but the child had a special aversion to watching the feats of trained wild animals, and had often shut her eyes when such a performance was going on.

The lions and tigers came in and took their places, and Kitty and King watched with interest as they obeyed the trainer's word, and did as he bade them.

But after a little time, Marjorie felt she could stand it no longer.
"Pomp," she said, "I can't bear to look at those animals another minute!
This is the last number, and I'm going out. I'll wait for you right by
the door, just where we came into the tent."
Pompton looked at the child, kindly. Her face was white, and he saw that it really distressed her to watch the wild animals.

"Very well, Miss Marjorie," he said; "it's but a few steps, so go on, if you like, and stay just outside the door until we come. Don't wander away now."

"No, Pompton, I won't wander away, but I must get away from here."

Marjorie left the box, and went quietly out of the door of the tent. It was only a few steps, as their box was very near the entrance.

There was a bench just outside the door, and the little girl sat down upon it, delighted to be away from the sights she did not care for. The fresh air and bright sunshine brought the color back to her cheeks, and she looked around her with interest. There was little to see, for the audience were all inside the great tent, and the performers were either on the stage or in their own dressing rooms. A pleasant-faced attendant spoke to her, and asked where her people were.

"They're inside," answered Marjorie, "they're coming out in a few moments, but I didn't like this act, and I'm going to wait for them here."

"All right, little one; sit there as long as you like. I'll be about here all the time, and if you want anything, you call me. My name's Bill."

"Thank you," said Marjorie, and Bill went off whistling. He was a big, burly young man, with a kind voice and manner, and he seemed to be a hard-working circus hand. He was clearing up the place, and once in a while he glanced at Marjorie, as if to make sure she was all right.

Marjorie sat still on the bench, her thoughts all on the performances she had seen. She wondered if the circus people were like other people, for they seemed to her to be of a different race.

As she was thinking, a young girl came out of a small tent nearby. She had a long cloak wrapped round her, but her gaily-dressed hair with silver stars pinned in it, made Marjorie feel sure she was one of the performers. She had a very pretty face, and she smiled pleasantly at Marjorie, as she said, "What are you doing here, little girl?"

"I'm waiting for my people," said Marjorie. "They're coming out in a minute, but I couldn't stand those fierce animals any longer."

"How funny," said the young lady, and she sat down in the seat beside Marjorie. "Do you know I always shiver when I look at the wild animals, too. I've been with the circus a year, and I can't get used to those lions and tigers. I always think they're going to spring at me, though I know perfectly well they're not. Is that the way you feel?"

"Yes, I feel just like that, and I know it's silly, but I can't help it.
What do you do in the circus?"
The girl partly flung open her long cloak, and disclosed her costume of spangled pink satin.

"I'm one of the trapeze performers; you probably saw me swing this afternoon."

"Oh, are you really one of those swinging ladies? Do tell me about it, won't you? Don't you get dizzy, swinging through the air upside down?"

"No, we never get dizzy; that would never do! Why, we'd fall and break our necks, and I assure you we don't want to do that!"

"Don't you ever fall?"

"Oh, of course accidents have happened, but much more rarely than most people think. Trapeze performers are a very careful lot, and we seldom have an accident."

"Are all those trapeze people your family?" asked Marjorie, for the troupe was billed as one family.

"Many of them are, but not all. I have one sister who is an acrobat. She is really one of the best I ever saw for her age. She's only twelve, and she can do wonderful feats for such a child."

"I'm twelve," said Marjorie, smiling, "but my brother says I'm too fat to do anything like that."

"Yes, you are," and the young lady smiled, showing her even, white teeth. She was a very pretty girl, and had a sweet, refined voice, which surprised Marjorie, as she had not thought circus people were like this.

"You do weigh too much to be very agile; my sister is slender, but very muscular. Would you like to see her? She's right over there in our tent, with Mother."

"Oh, I'd love to see her, but I mustn't go away from here, for I told
Pomp where to find me. He'll be out soon."
"Yes, the performance will be over in about five minutes. But I'd like you to see my sister. Her name is Vivian, and she's so sweet and pretty! But of course if you think you'd better stay here, I don't want to persuade you. I must go back now myself. We're really not allowed out here at this time."

Marjorie wanted very much to go in to the tent with the young lady, and to see the little sister, and she wondered if she could in any way get word to Pompton telling him where she was. Just then Bill came round that way again, and smiled at her.

"Oh, Bill," cried Marjorie, impulsively, "you said if I wanted anything to ask you. Now I want to go into the tent with this lady,—she says I may,—and won't you please go in the big tent, and tell my people where I've gone? You can't miss them, they're in Box number five. An Englishman named Pompton, who is our chauffeur,—and three children with him. Will you, Bill, 'cause I want to see this lady's little sister?"

"Sure, I'll 'tend to it, Miss. They won't let me in myself, but I'll fix it with the doorman, and it'll be all right. Why, bless you, the tent isn't a step away. Run along with Mademoiselle Cora."

"Is that your name? What a pretty name," said Marjorie, and giving
Mademoiselle Cora her hand, the two crossed over to the little tent.
CHAPTER XVII
LITTLE VIVIAN
It was about ten minutes later when Pompton and his three charges came out of the circus tent. There was a great crowd, and not seeing Marjorie at first, Pompton waited until most of the people had gone away, and then began to look around for her.

"I know she wouldn't go very far away," said King. "She must be quite near here."

"I'm not so sure," said Kitty. "You know how Marjorie runs off if she chooses, without thinking of other people."

"I'm greatly worried, Master King," said Pompton. "I suppose I ought not to have let the child come out here alone. But she was so anxious to come, and she promised she'd stay right here by the door. I couldn't come with her, and look after the rest of you at the same time now, could I?"

"Of course you couldn't, Pompton," said Kitty. "You did quite right. And I don't believe Marjorie is very far away; I think she'll be back in a minute or two."

But they waited several minutes, and the people who had been in the circus tent all went away. The grounds about were entirely cleared, and save for a few workmen, there was no one in sight. Uncertain what to do, Pompton appealed to the doorman, who just then came out with his hands full of tickets.

"Do you know anything about a little girl, about twelve years old, who came out of the tent a short time ago?" asked Pompton.

"Naw," returned the man, curtly, paying little attention to the inquiry.

"But you must have seen her come out," said King. "She came out alone, before the performance was over. She had on a long tan-colored coat."

"Aw, that kid? Yes, I seen her, but I don't know where she went to."

"But we must find her! She's my sister!" said Kitty, and the tears came into her eyes.

The doorman looked at Pompton. "You ought to keep yer kids together, an' not let yer party get sep'rated."

"It wasn't Pompton's fault at all!" cried King, indignantly. "My sister came out here to wait for us, and of course she's around here somewhere. She must be in one of the tents. May we go and look for her?"

"Sure! Go where you like. I s'pose she's pokin' around somewhere to see what's goin' on."

"Of course she's in one of the tents," said Kitty, brightening at the idea. "Where shall we look first, King?"

Just then the man named Bill came along.

"Hello, youngsters," he said. "Lookin' fer that kid sister of yours? She told me to tell you where she'd gone, but, bless my soul, I forgot all about it!"

"Oh, where is she?" cried Kitty, clasping her hands, and looking up at
Bill with pleading eyes.
"There, there, little one! There ain't no use gettin' weepy about it.
Sister's all right. She just went in that there tent with Mademoiselle
Cora."
Bill pointed to the tent, and King and Kitty made a dash for it.

They fairly burst in at the door, and sure enough, there was Marjorie sitting on a big packing box, watching a little girl who was performing most remarkable athletic feats.

"Oh, hello," cried Marjorie, "I'm so glad you've come! Just sit down here beside me, and watch Vivian. Mademoiselle Cora, this is my brother and sister."

King pulled off his cap, and felt a little uncertain as to what sort of etiquette this very strange situation demanded. But he bowed politely, and as Mademoiselle Cora smiled, and asked the two newcomers to be seated, and as there were plenty of packing boxes, King and Kitty sat down.

"This is Vivian," said Marjorie, waving her hand toward the little acrobat, who was turning double somersaults with lightning rapidity. "She's only twelve, isn't she wonderful?"

The experience was so novel, it is scarcely to be wondered at that King and Kitty fell under the spell, as Marjorie had done, and the three sat breathlessly watching Vivian.

Mademoiselle Cora smiled at the enraptured audience, and in a far corner of the tent sat a placid-looking woman knitting a shawl. This was the mother of the two girls, but she took little interest in the visitors, and except for an occasional glance at them, devoted herself to her knitting.

After waiting a few moments, and seeing that the children did not reappear, Pompton decided to go into the tent himself. He hesitated about taking Rosamond in, but there was no help for it, so carrying the child in his arms, he pushed aside the canvas flap which formed the tent door, and stepped inside.

"My word!" he exclaimed, as he saw the youthful performer, and the interested audience. "You children are the most surprising! I think you had better come away now."

"I think so, too," remarked Vivian's mother, looking up for a moment from her knitting. "Are there many more of you to come?"

"Now don't be uncivil, Mother," said Cora, with her pretty smile. "It does no harm for these children to see Vivian perform. You know she wasn't on the programme to-day."

"I'm only a beginner," said Vivian, standing on her feet once more, and speaking to Marjorie and Kitty. "I've had quite a good deal of training, and now I'm on the programme afternoons twice a week. Next year I'll be on every afternoon."

"Do you like it?" asked Kitty, fascinated by this strange child. Vivian was a pretty little girl, and she wore a garment of pink muslin, shaped like children's rompers. She wore pink stockings and pink kid sandals, and her golden hair was short, and curled all over her little head.

"Yes, I like it," replied Vivian, but a wistful look came into her blue eyes. Gently, almost timidly, she touched Marjorie's pretty coat and straw hat with her slender little fingers. "I like it,—but I think I'd rather be a little home-girl like you."

"Cora, send those children away," said the mother, sharply. "They upset Vivian completely when she sees them."
"I like to see them," said Vivian, and she sat down between Kitty and Midget. "I like to see your pretty dresses, and real shoes and stockings. Do you go to school?"

Marjorie felt strangely drawn to this little girl who seemed so to want the privacy of a home life. She spoke to her very gently. "Yes, Vivian, we all go to school,—though I don't go to a regular school, do you?"

"No, I don't. Mother and Cora say they'll teach me every day, while we're on the road, but they never get time. And I have to practise a great deal."

Marjorie looked around for a piano, and then suddenly realized that
Vivian meant she must practise her gymnastic exercises.
"Come, Miss Marjorie, we must be going," said Pompton, who felt moved himself by the pathetic face of the little circus girl.

"Well, perhaps you'd better go now," said Cora, who had received imperative glances from her mother. "But we've enjoyed seeing you, and we thank you for your call."

Mademoiselle Cora had very polite manners, but she seemed to be under the rule of her mother, and it was with evident reluctance that she bade the visitors good-bye.

"I'll give you my picture," said Vivian to Marjorie, as they parted, "because I want you to remember me. I would like to have your picture, but Mother won't let me have little girls' photographs. She thinks it makes me feel envious to see pictures of little home-girls."

"Well, I'll give you something to remember me by," said Marjorie, impulsively, and she took from her neck a string of blue beads, and clasped it round Vivian's throat.

"Oh, thank you," said Vivian, with sparkling eyes. "I shall wear them always, and love them because you gave them to me. Good-bye, dear, dear little home-girl!"

The tears came into Marjorie's eyes at the tremor in Vivian's voice, and she kissed her affectionately, and then bidding good-bye to Mademoiselle Cora they followed Pompton out of the tent.

They were all rather silent as they trudged along to the trolley-car, and then Kitty said slowly, "Isn't it awful to be like that? I suppose she never has any home-life at all."

"Of course she hasn't, Miss Kitty, as she has no home," said Pompton; "it's wicked to put a child like that in a circus, it certainly is! She's a sweet little girl, and her sister is a fine young lady, too."

"The mother is horrid," said King. "She was awful cross about our being there."

"Well," said Kitty, who sometimes saw deeper than the rest, "you mustn't blame her too much. Couldn't you see she didn't want us there, because just the sight of happy home-children makes little Vivian feel sorry that she has to live in a circus?"

"Yes, that was it," said Marjorie. "I suppose they haven't any other way to earn their living."

The children could scarcely wait to get home to tell their parents of this wonderful experience.

They found Mr. and Mrs. Maynard waiting for them at the hotel, and wondering a little because they were late.

"Oh," cried Marjorie, flinging herself into her mother's arms, "we've had a most 'stonishing time! We visited a little circus girl in her own tent, and here's her picture!"

Marjorie held up to her mother's amazed view the picture of little Vivian. It was taken in stage costume, and represented Vivian in one of her clever acrobatic feats. Her pretty child-face wore a sweet smile, and the whole effect of the photograph was dainty and graceful. Across a corner was scrawled the word "Vivian" in large, childish letters.

"Did you buy this?" asked Mrs. Maynard, knowing that circus performers often sold their photographs.

"Oh, no, indeed, Mother; she gave it to me. And what do you think, Mother? The poor little thing has to live in a tent, and she wants to live in a home! And it made her awful sad to see us, 'cause we have a home, and we can wear regular dresses and shoes, and she has to wear queer bloomer things,—and sandals on her feet!"

"But I don't understand, Marjorie," said Mrs. Maynard. "How do you know all this? Did you talk with the child?"

"Oh, yes, Mother; we went in her tent, and saw her mother and sister. I don't think they mind being in the circus so much. But Vivian feels just awful about it! And she's such a sweet little thing; and, Mother, I have the loveliest plan! Don't you think it would be nice for us to 'dopt her, and let her live with us?"

"Midget, what are you talking about?" and Mrs. Maynard's face showed so plainly her dissent to the proposition that Marjorie jumped out of her lap, and ran across to her father, in the hope of better success.

"Now, Father," she said as she threw her arms around his neck, and drew his arms around her; "do please pay 'tention to my plan! You know we ought to do some good in this world, and what could be better than rescuing a poor little sad circus girl, and letting her live in our own happy home with us? It wouldn't cost much,—she could have half of my clothes, and half of Kitty's,—we could each get along with half, I know. And we could both eat less,— that is, I could,—I don't know about Kit. But anyway, Father, won't you think about it?"

"Yes, dear," said Mr. Maynard, looking fondly at his impetuous daughter; "I'll think about it right now,—and I'll express my thoughts aloud, as I think them. I think, first, that you're a generous and kind-hearted little girl to want to give this poor child a home. And I think next, that having made your suggestion, you must leave it to Mother and me to decide the matter. And our decision is that four children are quite enough for this family, and we don't want to adopt any more! Besides this, Marjorie, it is far from likely that the little girl would be allowed to come to us. She is being trained for her profession, and though I feel sorry that the child is not happy, yet she is with her own people, and they are responsible for the shaping of her life and career. Just now, you are carried away by sympathy for the little girl, and I don't blame you at all, for it is a sad case. But you must trust your father's judgment, when he tells you that he does not think it wise to follow out your suggestion."

Marjorie looked disappointed, but she well knew that when her father talked thus seriously, there was no use in pursuing the subject; so she only said, "All right, Father; I know you know best. But it does seem too bad for Vivian not to have any home pleasures, when I have so many!"

"It does seem too bad, Marjorie, but since you can't help her in any way, turn your thoughts to feeling glad and grateful that you yourself have a happy home, and can wear button boots."

Marjorie laughed at her father's last words, but she knew that "button boots" stood for the civilized dress of the home-child, as contrasted with the stage trappings of the little Vivian.

So she put the photograph away among her treasures, and often looked at it, and wondered if Vivian still longed for the sort of happy home-life that meant so much to Marjorie.

CHAPTER XVIII
IN BOSTON

The next day the Maynards started for Boston. That is, their destination was Boston, but Mr. and Mrs. Maynard had decided to go by very short stages, and stop several times on the way.

And so they spent one night at New London, two or three more at Newport and Narragansett Pier, and so on to Boston.

It was too early in the season for the summer crowds at the watering places, but though the gay life was absent, they enjoyed their stay at each place.

It was all so novel to the children that the days passed like a swiftly moving panorama, and they went from one scene to another, always sure of experiencing some new pleasure.

* * * * *

One warm and pleasant afternoon the big car swung into Boston, and deposited its occupants at a pleasant hotel on a broad and beautiful avenue.

As Mr. Maynard registered at the office, the clerk handed him a budget of mail. It was not unusual for him to find letters awaiting him at the various hotels, but this time there were also four post-cards for the children.

"Who can have written to us?" exclaimed Marjorie, as she took hers. "I don't know this hand-writing; I'm sure I never saw it before."

She turned the card over, and saw a picture of the State House, one of
Boston's principal places of interest. Beneath the picture was written:
"Please come and visit me;
I am the place you want to see."
"How funny," said Marjorie. "Who could have sent it? Is it an advertisement, Father?"

"No, Midget, The State House doesn't have to advertise itself! What is yours, King?"

"Mine is a picture of the Public Library, and this has a verse under it, too. It says:

"How do you think you like my looks?
Beautiful pictures and wonderful books!"
"These are lots of fun, whoever sent them," said Kitty. "Listen to mine.
It's a picture of Faneuil Hall. Under it is written:
"Do not think you have seen all
Until you have visited Faneuil Hall!"
"And Rosy Posy has one, too," said Marjorie. "Let sister read it, dear."

"Yes, Middy wead my post-card," and the baby handed it over.

"This is a lovely one," said Marjorie. "See, it's all bright-colored flowers, and it says:

"The Boston Common's bright and gay,
With tulips in a brave array."
"Sure enough," said Mrs. Maynard, "the tulips must be in bloom now, and to-morrow we must go to see them."

"Oh, what lovely times we are having!" cried Marjorie. "How long are we going to stay in Boston, Father?"

"Long enough, at any rate, to see all these sights suggested by your post-cards. And I may as well tell you, children, that the cards were sent by Mr. Bryant, a friend of mine in Cambridge; and we are going to visit at his house when we leave here."

"Have we ever seen him?" asked Marjorie.

"Only when you were very small children; not since you can remember. But they are delightful people, and indeed are distant cousins of your mother. I can assure you you'll have a good time at their home."

"We seem to have good times everywhere," said Marjorie, with a happy little sigh of content. "This has been the most beautiful May ever was! And a real Maynard May, because we've all been together all the time!"

"May for the Maynards, and the Maynards for May," sang King, and they all repeated the line, which was one of their favorite mottoes.

"Maytime is a lovely time, anyway, isn't it, Father?" said Marjorie.

"Yes, unless it rains," Mr. Maynard replied, smiling.

"Well, we've had awful little rain since we started," commented Marjorie; "just a little shower now and then, and that's all."

"Maytime is playtime for us this year, sure enough," said her father; "I hope you children realize that these are all Ourdays, and you're piling up enough of them to last for two or three years ahead."

"Oh, they don't count that way, do they?" cried Kitty, in such dismay that her father laughed.

"Don't worry, Kitsie," he said. "I guess we can squeeze out a few Ourdays in the future. Meantime, enjoy your Maytime while you may."

And this the Maynard family proceeded to do. They spent several days in Boston, seeing the sights of the town, and making little excursions to the suburbs and nearby places of interest.

They visited the Public Library, and studied the wonderful paintings there. They went to the State House, and Faneuil Hall, and Mr. Maynard showed the children so many interesting relics, and taught them so much interesting New England history that Marjorie declared he was quite as good a teacher as Miss Hart.

They spent much time in the Public Gardens and on the Common, for the Maynard children dearly loved to be out of doors, and the flowers in their masses of bloom were enchanting.

Indeed, there was so much of interest to see that Marjorie felt almost sorry when the time came to go to Cambridge for their visit at Mr. and Mrs. Bryant's. But her father told her that on their return from Cambridge they could, if they wished, spend a few more days in Boston. And so, one afternoon, the Maynards drove away from the hotel in their car, and crossed the Charles River to Cambridge.

The Bryants' home was a fine, large estate not far from Harvard College.

"Another college!" exclaimed Marjorie, as they passed the University Buildings. "Can we go through this one, Father, as we did through Yale?"
"Yes," said Mr. Maynard, "and then King can make a choice of which he wants to attend."

"I think I know already," returned King; "but I won't tell you yet, for I may change my mind."

As they turned in at the gateway of the Bryants' home they found themselves on a long avenue, bordered with magnificent trees. This led to the house, and on the veranda their host and hostess stood awaiting them.

"You dear people! I'm so glad to see you; jump right out, and come in," exclaimed Mrs. Bryant, as the car stopped. She was a pretty, vivacious little lady, with cordial hospitality beaming from her gray eyes, and Mr. Bryant, a tall, dark-haired man, was no less enthusiastic in his greetings.

"Hello, Ed," he cried. "Mighty glad to see you here! Hope we can give you a good time! I know we can make it pleasant for you grownups, but it's the kiddies I'm thinking about. I told Ethel she must just devote herself to their entertainment all the time they're here. She's

95

laid in a lot of playthings for them, and they must just consider that the house is their own, and they can do whatever they like from attic to cellar! How many? Four? That's what I thought. I don't know their names, but I'll learn them later. Here, jump up, Peter, Susan, Mehitabel,—or whatever your names are,—and let me see how you look!"

As jovial Mr. Bryant had been talking, he had lifted the children from the car. He paid little attention to them individually, seeming to think they were mere infants.

Mrs. Bryant was chatting away at the same time. "Is this Marjorie?" she said. "My, what a big girl! When I last saw her she was only six or seven. And Kingdon,—almost a young man, I declare! Kitty, I remember,—but this little chunk of sweetness I never saw before!"

She picked up Rosy Posy in her arms, and the little one smiled and patted her cheek, for Mrs. Bryant had a taking way with children, and they always loved her.

Marjorie couldn't help thinking what a contrast this greeting was to their reception at Grandma Maynard's, but she also realized that the Bryants were much younger people, and apparently were very fond of children.

Altogether, it was a most satisfactory welcome, and the Maynards trooped into the house, with that comfortable feeling always bestowed by a warm reception.

"Now, I'll take you girlies upstairs," Mrs. Bryant chatted on, taking Marjorie and Kitty each by a hand; "and I'll brush your hair and wash your paddies, and fix you up all nice for supper."

Marjorie couldn't help laughing at this.

"Don't let us make you too much trouble, Mrs. Bryant," she said. "You know we're quite big girls, and we tie each other's ribbons."

"Bless me! Is that so? But you musn't call me Mrs. Bryant! I'm Cousin Ethel, and Mr. Bryant is Cousin Jack, and if you call us anything more formal than that, we'll feel terribly offended!"

And then Cousin Ethel bustled away to look after her other guests, leaving Midget and Kitty to take care of themselves.

She had given them a delightful room, large and sunshiny, with a sort of a tower bay-window on one corner. The carpet was sprinkled with little rosebuds, and the wall-paper matched it. Some of the chairs and the couch were covered with chintz, and that, too, had little rosebuds all over it. The curtains at the windows were of frilled white muslin, and the dressing table had all sorts of dainty and pretty appointments. There were twin brass beds, and on the foot of each was a fluffy, rolled coverlet, with more pink rosebuds.

"What a darling room!" exclaimed Marjorie, as she looked around. "Oh,
Kit, isn't it pretty?"
"Lovely!" agreed Kitty. "And Cousin Ethel is a darling, too. I love her already! We're going to have a beautiful time here, Mops."

"Yes, indeedy! I wish we were going to stay all summer. Kit, this is a perfect May room, isn't it?"

"Yes, it's so flowery and bright. What are we going to wear, Mops?"

"White dresses, I s'pose. Our trunk is here, you see."

"And let's wear our Dresden sashes and ribbons,—then we'll match this rosebuddy room."

And so when Cousin Ethel returned to her young guests, she found them all spick and span, in their dainty white frocks and pretty ribbons.

"Bless your sweet hearts!" she cried, kissing them both. "You look like Spring Beauties! Come on downstairs with me."
She put an arm around each of the girls, and they all went down the broad staircase. In the hall below they met Cousin Jack, who looked at them with an expression of disappointment on his face.

"Well!" he said. "Well, Susan and Mehitabel,—I'm surprised at you!"

"What's the matter?" asked Marjorie, who could not imagine what Cousin Jack meant. Kitty, too, looked disturbed, for since Cousin Ethel had approved of their pretty dresses, she could not think what Cousin Jack was criticising.

"The idea," he went on, "of you girls coming down dressed like that!"

"What do you mean, Jack?" asked his wife, "I'm sure these darlings look lovely."

"Yes, they do," and Mr. Bryant's tone was distinctly aggrieved; "but, you see, I thought we'd play Indians,—and who could play Indians with such dressed-up poppets as these?"

Cousin Ethel laughed. "Oh, that's all right," she said. "Of course you can't play Indians to-night, but you can play it all day to-morrow. And now, I think supper is ready. We usually have dinner at night, but we're having supper on account of you children."

"You're awfully good to us, Cousin Ethel," said Marjorie, appreciatively.
"We do sit up to dinner at home, unless there are guests."
"Well, I'll see that you get enough to eat, whether it's supper or dinner," Cousin Jack assured them, and then, the others having arrived, they all went to the dining-room.

The supper, besides being substantial and satisfying, seemed to include almost everything that appealed to the children's tastes; and when at last the ice cream appeared, Kitty's look of supreme content convinced Cousin Ethel that the meal had been wisely ordered.

After supper they all went into the large living room, and Cousin Jack proceeded to entertain them.

"At what time do you have to go to bed, Mehitabel?" he asked of Marjorie, whom, for no reason at all, he persisted in calling by that ridiculous name.

"They must go by nine o'clock," said Mrs. Maynard, answering the question herself. "The three older ones may sit up until then."

"All right, Madam Maynard; then I shall devote my attention to the three until their bedtime, after which I may be able to chat a little while with you and Ed."

Cousin Jack was as good as his word, and entertained the children zealously until nine o'clock. He arranged a magic lantern show, and as the pictures were very funny, and Cousin Jack's description of them funnier still, the young Maynards were kept in peals of laughter, in which the older part of the audience often joined.

After this, he let them listen to a large talking-machine, and as many of the records were humorous songs or comical dialogues, there was more laughter and hilarity.

Nine o'clock came all too soon, and the children trooped off to bed, regretfully.

"Shoo!" cried Cousin Jack, as the clock struck, "shoo, every one of you!
Scamper, Mehitabel! Fly, Susannah! And hustle, Hezekiah!"
With Cousin Jack clapping his hands and issuing his peremptory orders, the children ran laughing away, and scurried upstairs.

"Did you ever see such ducky people?" said King, as he lingered in the upper hall a minute with his sisters.

"They're perfectly beautiful!" said Marjorie. "And I can hardly wait for to-morrow to come to see what Cousin Jack will do next."

"Let's go to bed," said practical Kitty, "and that'll make to-morrow come quicker. Good-night, King."

"Good-night, Kit; good-night, Mopsy," and with an affectionate tweak of his sisters' curls. King went away to his own room, and the girls to theirs.

CHAPTER XIX
FUN AT COUSIN ETHEL'S
Next morning Midget and Kitty were awake early, and found that the sunshine was fairly pouring itself in at their bay window.

"I don't believe it's time to get up," said Midget, as she smiled at
Kitty across the room.
"No; Mother said she'd call us when it was time," returned Kitty, cuddling down under her rosebudded coverlet.

But just then something flew in at the open window, and landed on the floor between their two beds.

"What's that?" cried Marjorie, startled. And then she saw that it was a large red peony blossom. It was immediately followed by another, and that by a branch of lilac blooms. Then came hawthorn flowers, syringa, Rose of Sharon, roses, bluebells, and lots of other flowers, and sprays of green, until there was a perfect mound of flowers in the middle of the room, and stray blossoms fallen about everywhere.

"It's Cousin Jack, of course," cried Marjorie. "Let's get up, Kit."

The girls sprang out of bed, and throwing on their kimonas, ran and peeped out of the window, from behind the curtains.

Sure enough, Cousin Jack was standing down on the lawn, and when he saw the smiling faces, he began to chant a song to them:

"Susannah and Mehitabel, come out and play!
 For it's a lovely, sunny, shiny day in May;
 And Cousin Jack is waiting here for you,
 So hurry up, and come along, you two!"
Marjorie and Kitty could dress pretty quickly when they wanted to, so they were soon ready, and in fresh pink gingham dresses and pink hair-ribbons, they ran downstairs and out on to the lawn. King was already there, for Cousin Jack had roused him also.

"Hello, Kiddy-widdies!" Cousin Jack called out, as the girls flew toward him. "However did you get bedecked in all this finery so quickly?"

"This isn't finery," said Kitty; "these are our morning frocks. But say, Cousin Jack, how did you manage to throw those flowers in at our window from down here?"

"Oh, I'm a wizard; I can throw farther than that."

"Yes, a ball," agreed Marjorie; "but I don't see how you could throw flowers."

"Oh, I just gave them to the fairies, and they threw them in," and Cousin Jack wouldn't tell them that really he had thrown them from a nearby balcony, and gone down to the lawn afterward.

"Well, anyway, it was a lovely shower of flowers, and we thank you lots," said Marjorie.

"You're a nice, polite little girl, Mehitabel, and I'm glad to see you don't forget your manners. Now we have a good half hour before breakfast, what shall we play?"

Kitty sidled over to Cousin Jack, and whispered, a little timidly, "You said we'd play Indians."

"Bless my soul! A gentle little thing like you, Susannah, wanting to play Indians! Well, then that's what we play. I'll be the Chief, and my name is Opodeldoc. You two girls can be squaws,—no, you needn't either. Mehitabel can be a Squaw, and Susannah, you are a pale-

99

faced Maiden, and we'll capture you. Then Hezekiah here can be a noble young Brave, who will rescue you from our clutches! His name will be Ipecacuanha."

Surely Cousin Jack knew how to play Indians! These arrangements suited the young Maynards perfectly, and soon the game was in progress. The Indian Chief and the Squaw waited in ambush for the pale-faced Maiden to come along; the Chief meanwhile muttering dire threats of terrible tortures.

Throwing herself into the game with dramatic fervor, Kitty came strolling along. She hummed snatches of song, she paused here and there to pick a flower, and as she neared the bush behind which the two Indians were hiding, she stopped as if startled. Shading her eyes with her hand, she peered into the bush, exclaiming, in tragic accents, "Methinks I hear somebody! It may be Indians in ambush! Yes, yes,—that is an ambush, there must be Indians in it!"

This speech so amused Cousin Jack that he burst into shouts of laughter.

Kitty, absorbed in her own part, did not smile. "Hah!" she exclaimed, "methinks I hear the Indians warwhooping!"

Kitty's idea of dramatic diction was limited to "Hah!" and "Methinks," and after this speech, Cousin Jack gave way to a series of terrific warwhoops, in which Marjorie joined. Cousin Jack was pretty good at this sort of thing, but his lungs gave out before Marjorie's did, for, this being her specialty, her warwhoops were of a most extreme and exaggerated nature.

"Good gracious, Mehitabel, do hush up!" cried the Indian Chief, clapping his hand over his Squaw's mouth. "You'll have all the neighbors over here, and the police and the fire department! Moderate your transports! Warwhoop a little less like a steam calliope!"

Marjorie giggled, and then gave a series of small, squeaky, lady-like warwhoops, which seemed to amuse Cousin Jack as much as the others had done.

"You are certainly great kids!" he exclaimed. "I'd like to buy the whole bunch of you! But come on, my Squaw, we waste time, and the pale-faced Maiden approacheth. Hah!"

"Hah!" replied Marjorie, and from behind his own distant ambush, King muttered, "Hah!"

Kitty stood patiently waiting to be captured, and so Chief Opodeldoc hissed between his teeth, "Hah! the time is ripe! Dash with me, oh, Squaw, and let us nab the paleface!"

"Dash on! I follow!" said Marjorie, and with a mad rush, the two fierce
Indians dashed out from behind their bush, and captured the pale-faced
Maiden.
Kitty struggled and shrieked in correct fashion, while the Indians danced about her, brandishing imaginary tomahawks, and shrieking moderately loud warwhoops.

The terrified paleface was just about to surrender, when the noble young Brave, Ipecacuanha, dashed forth, and sprang into the fray, rescuing the maiden just in the nick of time. Holding the paleface, who lay limp and gasping in his left arm, the young Indian madly fought the other two of his own tribe with his strong right arm. Apparently he, too, had a tomahawk, for he fearfully brandished an imaginary weapon, and did it so successfully, that Opodeldoc and his faithful Squaw were felled to the ground. Then the brave young Indian and the fair girl he had saved from her dire fate danced a war dance round their prostrate captives, and chanted a weird Indian dirge, that caused the fallen Chief to sit up and roar with laughter.

"You children do beat all!" he exclaimed once more. "And, by jiminy crickets! there goes the breakfast bell! Are you wild Indians fit to appear in a civilized dining-room?"

"'Course we are!" cried Marjorie, jumping up and shaking her frills into place. Kitty stood demurely beside her, and sure enough, the two girls were quite fresh and dainty enough for breakfast.

"You see," explained Marjorie, "this wasn't a real tumble around play. Sometimes when we play Indians, we lose our hair-ribbons and even tear our frocks, but to-day we've behaved pretty well, haven't we, King?"

"Yep," assented her brother, looking at the girls critically, "you look fine. Am I all right?"

"Yes," said Marjorie, as she smoothed down one refractory lock at the back of his head. "We're all ready, Cousin Jack." She turned a smiling face toward him, and remarking once again, "You do beat all!" the ex-Chief marched his young visitors in to breakfast.

After that delightful and very merry meal was over, Cousin Ethel announced that she would take charge of the two girls that morning, and that King could share in their occupation or not as he chose.

"You see, it's this way, girlies," said Cousin Ethel, after she had led the way to a pleasant corner of the veranda, and her guests were grouped about her. "A Charity Club to which I belong is going to have a sort of an entertainment which is not exactly a fair or a bazaar, but which is called a Peddler's Festival. Of course, it is to make money for charity, and while the older people have charge of it, they will be assisted by young people, and even children. Now I think it will be lovely for you chick-a-biddies to take part in this affair, if you want to; but if you don't want to, you must say so frankly, for you're not going to do anything you don't like while your Cousin Ethel is on deck!"

"S'pose you tell 'em about it, Ethelinda, and let them judge for themselves," said her husband, who was sitting on the veranda railing, with Midge and Kitty on either side of him, and Rosamond in his arms.

"Well, it's this way," began Cousin Ethel. "Instead of having articles for sale in any room or hall, we are going to send them all around town, in pushcarts or wagons, each in charge of a peddler. These peddlers will be young people dressed in fancy costumes, and each will try to sell his load of wares by calling from house to house. Some peddlers will have pushcarts or toy express wagons, or even wheelbarrows. Others will carry a suitcase or a basket or a peddler's pack. They may go together or separately, and the whole day will be devoted to it."

"Great scheme!" commented Cousin Jack. "Wish we might be in it, eh, Ned?"

"Well, no," said Mr. Maynard, "I don't believe I care about that sort of thing myself, but I rather think the Maynard chicks will like it."

"Yes, indeed," cried Marjorie, her eyes dancing at the thought; "I think it will be lovely fun, Cousin Ethel. But can we girls push a big pushcart? Do you mean like the grocers use?"

"There will be a few of those," said Cousin Ethel, "and in all cases where the vehicles are too heavy for the girls, there will be young men appointed to do the pushing, while the girls cajole the customers into buying. It will not be difficult, as everybody will be waiting for you with open hearts and open purses."

"It's a grand plan," said Kitty, speaking with her usual air of thoughtful deliberation. "What shall we sell, Cousin Ethel?"

"Well, I'm undecided whether to put you two girls together, or put you each with some one else. I'd like to put you each with another little girl, but if I do that, I will have to put Marjorie with Bertha Baker, and I know she won't like it."

"Why won't she like it?" asked Marjorie, innocently. "I'll be nice to her."

"Bless your heart, you sweet baby, I don't mean that!" cried Cousin Ethel; "but the truth is, nobody likes Bertha Baker. She is a nice child in many ways, but she is,—"

"Grumpy-natured," put in Cousin Jack; "that's what's the matter with Bertha,—she hasn't any sunshine in her makeup. Now as Marjorie has sunshine enough for two, I think it will be a good plan to put them together."

"The plan is good enough," said his wife, "if Marjorie doesn't mind. But I don't want her pleasure spoiled because she has to be with a grumpy little girl. How about it, Marjorie?"

"I don't mind a bit," said Midget. "We're always good-natured ourselves, somehow we just can't help being so. And if Bertha Baker is cross, I'll just giggle until she has to giggle too."

"That's right, Midget," said her father, nodding his head approvingly. "And if you giggle enough, I think you'll make the grumpy Bertha merry before she knows it."

"You see," said Cousin Ethel, "everybody else is arranged for. And unless Marjorie goes with Bertha Baker, the child will have to go alone, for nobody else is willing to go with her."

"What a disagreeable girl she must be!" said King. "I'm glad I don't have to go with her."

"But you will have to, King," said Marjorie. "He'll have to push our cart, won't he, Cousin Ethel?"

"Why, yes, I thought he would do that; but he shan't if he doesn't want to."

"Oh, I do want to," declared King, agreeably. "I'm not afraid of any grumpy girl. I'll smile on her so sweetly, she'll have to smile back." And King gave such an idiotic grin that they all smiled back at him.

"Now," went on Cousin Ethel, briskly, "I thought, Marjorie, you could have the doll cart, and Kitty could be with May Perry and help sell the flowers. The flower wagon will be very pretty, and flowers are always easy to sell."

"So are dolls," said Marjorie. "Can I help you make some. Cousin Ethel, or are they already made?"

"The more elaborate dolls are being dressed by the ladies of our Club. But I thought, that if your mother and I and you girls could get to work to-day, we could make a lot of funny little dolls that I'm sure would be saleable."

"Let me help, too," said Cousin Jack. "I can make lovely dolls out of peanuts."

"Nonsense," said his wife, "we can all make peanut dolls. And besides, Jack, you must get away to your business. Your office boy will think you're lost, strayed, or stolen."

"I suppose I must," sighed Cousin Jack; "it's awful to be a workingman.
Come on, Ned; want to go in to Boston with me?"
The two men went away, and after a while Cousin Ethel called the children to come to what she called a Dolly-Bee.

On the table, in the pleasant living room, they found heaps of materials. Bits of silk and lace and ribbon, to dress little dolls,—and all sort of things to make dolls of.

King insisted on helping also, for he said he was just as handy about such things as the girls were. To prove this, he asked Cousin Ethel for a clothespin, and with two or three Japanese paper napkins, and a gay feather to stick in its cap, he cleverly evolved a very jolly little doll, whose features he made with pen and ink on the head of the clothespin.

And then they made dolls of cotton wadding, and dolls of knitting cotton, and peanut dolls, and Brownie dolls, and all sorts of queer and odd dolls which they invented on the spur of the moment.

They made a few paper dolls, but these took a great deal of time, so they didn't make many. Paper dolls were Kitty's specialty. But she cut them so carefully, and painted them so daintily, that they were real works of art, and therefore consumed more time than Cousin Ethel was willing to let her spend at the work.

"You mustn't tire yourselves out doing these," she admonished them. "I only want you to work at them as long as you enjoy it."

But the Maynards were energetic young people, and when interested, they worked diligently; and the result was they accumulated a large number of dolls to sell at the Festival.

King was given his choice between pushing a tinware cart with another boy, or pushing the doll cart for the girls.

He chose the latter, "because," said he, "I can't leave Mopsy to the tender mercies of that grumpy girl. And I don't think tinware is much fun, anyhow."

"How do we know where to go. Cousin Ethel?" said Marjorie, who was greatly interested in the affair.

"Oh, you just go out into the streets, and stop at any house you like. There won't be any procession. Every peddler goes when and where he chooses, until all his goods are sold."

"Suppose we can't sell them?" said Kitty.

"There's no danger of that. They're all inexpensive wares, and the whole population of Cambridge is expecting you, and the people are quite ready to spend their money for the good of the cause"

CHAPTER XX
THE FESTIVAL
Fortunately, the day of the Festival was a perfectly beautiful, balmy, lovely spring day. The affair had been well-advertised by circulars, and the residents of Cambridge had laid in a stock of small change, with which to buy the wares of the itinerant peddlers.

All was bustle and merriment at the Bryant home. The children were to start from there at about ten o'clock, and they were now getting on their costumes.

Each peddler was expected to dress appropriately to the character of the goods he was selling. This was not always an easy matter, but much latitude was allowed; and so a Greek peddler sold pastry, an Italian peddler sold peanuts, and an Indian Chief sold baskets and little Indian trinkets. There were many others, selling notions, fruits, and even fresh vegetables. One boy trundled a peanut roaster, and another was a vendor of lemonade.

When ready to start, the Maynard children and their carts presented a pretty appearance. The dolls were arranged in a light pushcart, borrowed from the grocer. It was decorated with frills of crêpe paper, and big paper bows at the corners. In it were more than a hundred dolls, ranging from the elaborately-dressed French beauties to the funny little puppets the children had made.

Marjorie and Bertha Baker were themselves dressed to represent dolls. Marjorie's dress was of pink muslin, frilled with lace, and a broad pink sash, tied low, with a big bow in the back. A frilled bonnet of pink muslin and lace crowned her dark curls, and she had been instructed by Cousin Ethel to walk stiffly, and move jerkily like a jointed doll. Bertha's costume was exactly like Marjorie's except that it was blue, and as Bertha's hair was blonde and curly, she looked very like a Bisque doll. But Bertha's face wore naturally a discontented expression, which was far less doll-like than Marjorie's smiling countenance.

As Cousin Ethel had prophesied, Marjorie found her new acquaintance decidedly ill-natured. But forewarned is forearmed, and Marjorie only replied pleasantly when Bertha made a sullen remark. Of course she was not really rude, and of course she had no reason to dislike Marjorie. But she was continually complaining that she was tired, or that the sun was too hot, or that she didn't like their cart as well as some of the others. She had an unfortunate disposition, and had not had the right training, so the result made her anything but an amiable child.

Gay-hearted Marjorie, however, joked with Bertha, and then giggled at her own jokes, until Bertha was really forced to smile in return.

King, who pushed the doll-cart, was also dressed like a doll. The boy looked very handsome, in a black velvet suit with lace ruffles at the wrists and knees, and long white stockings with black slippers. He was clever, too, in assuming the character, and walked with stiff, jerky strides, like a mechanical doll that had just been wound up.

Kitty was a dream of beauty. She was a little flower girl, of course, and wore the daintiest sort of a Dolly Varden costume. Her overdress of flowered muslin was caught up at the sides in panniers over a quilted skirt of light blue satin. A broad-brimmed leghorn hat with a wreath of roses, and fluttering blue ribbons, sat jauntily on her golden hair. May Perry, who was Kitty's companion, was costumed the same way, and the boy who pushed their cart was dressed like a page.

The flower cart held not only bouquets and old-fashioned nosegays, but little potted plants as well.

Cousin Jack had stayed home from business for the day; for, he said, he couldn't get away from the glories of his bevy of young people.

"Before you go," he said, as the two carts, with their attendants, were ready to start from his house, "I'll take a snap-shot of you."

He brought out his large camera, and took several photographs of the pretty group, which, later, proved to be beautiful pictures, and well worthy of framing.

"Now, go ahead, young peddlers," he said. "And whatever you do, remember to charge enough for your wares,—but don't charge too much."

"How shall we know what is just right?" asked Kitty, puckering her brow, as she pondered this knotty question.

"Well, Kit, if you're in doubt, leave it to the buyers. They'll probably give you more that way, than if you set the price yourself. And especially with flowers. People always expect to overpay for them at a fair."

"But I don't want to cheat the people," said Kitty.

"Don't worry about that; they quite expect to pay more than this trumpery is worth, because it's all for charity. Now skip along, my hearties! And come back home if you get tired, no matter whether you've sold all your truck or not. I'll buy whatever you have left."

So waving good-byes to the group looking after them, the children pranced gaily down the driveway and out into the street.

As Cousin Ethel had told them, they had no trouble at all in disposing of their wares. Marjorie concluded that half the population of Cambridge must be small children, so eager did the ladies seem to buy dolls.

At many of the houses they were cordially invited to come in and partake of some refreshment, for the whole town seemed bent on entertaining the peddlers. But the Maynard children preferred not to accept these invitations, as they were not well enough acquainted, and as for Bertha Baker, when she was invited in to a house, she would reply bluntly, "No, I don't want to go in."

Midget and King looked at her in astonishment, for they were not accustomed to hear children talk like that.

When the cart full of dolls had been about half sold, the children saw a little girl coming toward them with an empty express wagon.

"Hello, Bertha," she said, "what are you selling?"

"Dolls," said Bertha, shortly, and the Maynard children waited, expecting that Bertha would introduce the stranger.

But Bertha didn't, and only said, "Come on," to her own companions, and started on herself.

"Wait a minute," said King, who was growing rather tired of Bertha's company, and was glad to meet somebody else. "I say, Bertha, introduce us to your friend."

"She's Elsie Harland," said Bertha, ungraciously, and evidently unwillingly.

But King took no notice of Bertha's unpleasant manner. "How do you do, Elsie?" he said, in his frank, boyish fashion. "This is my sister, Marjorie, and I am Kingdon Maynard. Can't I help you pull your wagon? I see you've sold all your things."
"Yes; I only had post-cards to sell," said Elsie, "and the people bought them in such big bunches that now they're all gone. So I thought I'd like to go around with you, and help sell your dolls." She looked inquiringly at Bertha, who replied, "I s'pose you can, if you want to, but I should think you'd go home."

"Don't go home," said Marjorie, cordially; "come along with us, and we'll all sell dolls together."

"She can't sell our dolls," said Bertha, snappily, and this so irritated

King that he couldn't help speaking out.

"Bertha Baker," he said, "if you don't behave yourself, and act more pleasant, I'll put you in the cart, and sell you for a doll!"

This so surprised Bertha that she stared at King, wonderingly, but the other girls laughed, and then they all went on together.

Bertha made no further objections, and Marjorie could see that she did try to be a little more pleasant. King saw this, too, and he realized that she was the kind of a girl who obeyed scolding better than coaxing. So when they reached the next house, King said, "Now we'll all go in here together to sell the dolls; but we won't go until Bertha puts on a sweet smile. So, smile away, my lady!"

King's merry speech made Bertha laugh, and the dimples came in her cheeks, and she looked very pretty as they went up the walk.

"Goodness, Bertha!" exclaimed Elsie. "If you knew how much prettier you look when you smile, you'd always wear a broad grin!"

Bertha scowled at this, and seeing it, King stopped stock-still.

"Cook up that smile again!" he cried. "Not another step till you do!"

As the lady of the house was waiting for them on the veranda, this was embarrassing, so Bertha smiled, and then the whole group moved on.

So they kept on for the rest of the trip, King jollying Bertha whenever it was necessary, and the other girls making merriment for themselves. Marjorie and Elsie soon became friends, for they were alike merry-hearted and pleasant-mannered.

It was about noon when they sold their last doll and turned their faces homeward. Elsie and Bertha went with them, and when they reached Cousin Jack's house they found Kitty and May Perry already there.

"Here you are, my little peddlers! Here you are, with your empty carts!" cried Cousin Jack, as the children came upon the veranda. "All sold out, I see."

"Yes," said Marjorie, "and we could have sold more if we had had them."

"Then there's nothing left for me to buy from you, and I really need a doll."

"I'll make you one before I go home, Cousin Jack," said Marjorie; "and then you can keep it to remember me by."

"All right, Mehitabel; good for you! I'll play with it every day,—and when I go to see my little friends I'll take it with me. And now, my weary peddlers, let me tell you what you have still before you! A number of young people, mostly retired peddlers, are coming here to luncheon with you. But we won't call it luncheon, because that sounds so prosaic. We'll call it,—what shall we call it?"

"A festival feast," said Kitty. "That sounds gay and jolly."

"So it does," agreed Cousin Jack, "A May Day Festival Feast for the Maynards, and nothing could be pleasanter nor that!"
And even before Cousin Jack finished speaking, the young guests began to arrive, and Marjorie realized that it was a party her kind cousins had made for them.

There were about twenty guests all together, and as they wore the pretty costumes they had worn as peddlers, it was a picturesque group.

"Ho, for the Festival Feast!" exclaimed Cousin Jack, and taking Marjorie and Kitty by either hand he went dancing with them across the lawn.

Under a clump of trees they discovered that a table had been set, though it had not been visible from the house.

The table was like a vision of Fairyland, and Marjorie thought she had never before seen such a pretty one.

The decorations were of pink, and in the middle of the table was a wicker pushcart of fairly good size, filled with parcels wrapped in pink tissue paper. From each parcel a long end of ribbon led to the plate of each little guest. Also at each place was a much smaller pushcart of gilded wicker-work tied with pink bows, and filled with candies.

Pink sweet peas and ferns were scattered over the white tablecloth, and across the table ran a broad pink satin ribbon which bore in gold letters the legend, "May for the Maynards, the Maynards for May!"

"What a beautiful table!" cried Marjorie, as the lovely sight greeted her eyes.

"What beautiful guests!" cried Cousin Jack, as he looked at the smiling, happy crowd of children. And then he helped them to find their places, which were marked by pretty cards, painted with pink flowers.

As far as possible, everything was trimmed with pink. The china was white with pink bands, the rolled sandwiches were tied with little pink ribbons, the little cakes were iced with pink, and there were pink candies, and pink ice cream, and pink lemonade.

Then after the feast was over, the children were instructed to pull gently on the ribbons that lay at their plate, and thus draw toward them the pink paper parcels.

These being opened proved to contain a dainty gift for each one, the prevailing color, of course, being pink.

"It's the pinkiest party I ever saw!" exclaimed Marjorie. "It makes it seem more like May, being so pinky!"

"That's because it's for the Pink of Perfection," said Cousin Jack, looking fondly at Marjorie, whom he considered his chief guest.

Then they all left the table, and with Cousin Jack as ringleader, they played merry games until late in the afternoon.

At last the children all went home, and Marjorie threw her arms around Cousin Jack's neck, in a burst of gratitude. "You are too good to us!" she exclaimed.

"Now, Mehitabel, you know I think nothing could be too good for you, you're such a gay little Maynard! Can't I induce you to stay here with me when your people go home to-morrow?"

Marjorie laughed, for this was the second invitation she had had to leave her family. But she well knew Cousin Jack didn't expect her to do it, and so she smiled, and said, "I couldn't be induced to do that, Cousin Jack; but I think it would be awfully nice if you and Cousin Ethel would come and live in Rockwell. Then we could see you so much oftener."

"I'm not sure that we can go and live there,—but if we were coaxed very hard, we might come and visit you same time."

"I rather think you will!" said Mr. Maynard, heartily, "and the sooner you come, and the longer you stay, the better we'll like it!"

And before the Maynards left Cambridge, it was definitely arranged that
Cousin Jack and Cousin Ethel should visit them in the near future.
The next day the Maynards started for home. They were to stop a day or two in Boston, and then proceed by easy stages back to Rockwell.

As the big car started away from the Bryant house, after farewells both merry and affectionate, the children sang in gay chorus, one of their favorite road songs:

"All through the May
The Maynards play;
And every day
Is a holiday.
Glad and gay,
The Maynards play;
Maytime for Maynards,
Maynards for May!
No longer in Cambridge can we stay,
But over the hills and far-a-way;
And so good-day,
For we must away,
May for the Maynards! The Maynards for May!"

Note from the Editor

Odin's Library Classics strives to bring you unedited and unabridged works of classical literature. As such, this is the complete and unabridged version of the original English text unless noted. In some instances, obvious typographical errors have been corrected. This is done to preserve the original text as much as possible. The English language has evolved since the writing and some of the words appear in their original form, or at least the most commonly used form at the time. This is done to protect the original intent of the author. If at any time you are unsure of the meaning of a word, please do your research on the etymology of that word. It is important to preserve the history of the English language.

Taylor Anderson